MW00460165

DAWN LEE MCKENNA'S

AWASH

A *FORGOTTEN COAST* SUSPENSE NOVEL:
BOOK SIX

2016

A SWEET TEA PRESS PUBLICATION

First published in the United States by Sweet Tea Press

©2016 Dawn Lee McKenna. All rights reserved.

Edited by Tammi Labrecque
larksandkatydids.com

Cover by Shayne Rutherford
darkmoongraphics.com

Interior Design by Colleen Sheehan
wdrbookdesign.com

Awash is a work of fiction. All incidents and dialogue, and all characters, are products of the author's imagination. Any similarities to any person, living or dead, is merely coincidental.

No part of this publication may be reproduced, stored in a retrieval system, or transmitted in any form or by any means, electronic, mechanical, photocopying, recording, or otherwise, without the prior permission of the publishers.

For my fellow survivors
Touched but unbroken

-and for-

F-100 Lt. Jonathan Riley 1973-2014
-and-

F-112 Deputy Quinnaland Rhodes 1968-2012
who served Franklin County bravely and faithfully to the end

CHAPTER ONE

A brisk breeze that bordered on wind blew through the leaves of the old oak trees in the yard, and passed noisily through and around the palmettos and younger oaks in the woods across the street.

The old glass jalousie windows were open, and the girl sat on the loveseat just beneath the living room window so that she could hear the leaves more clearly, feel an occasional finger of cool, dry air tickle the back of her cocoa-colored neck.

There weren't many true autumn days in Apalachicola, FL, and perhaps this was one reason that those days were the girl's favorites. On this night, halfway between midnight and morning, the girl could close her eyes and believe that she was in one of those places she'd seen on TV, those places where the ground was covered with golden leaves and people had bonfires and cut their own Christmas trees. People with parents and cozy houses and clean, friendly dogs.

The girl closed the fat anatomy book she'd been reading, using her spiral notebook as a bookmark, and pushed it onto the cushion beside her. Usually, she could go to bed once her aunt came home from work or the bar, once she and the cats weren't alone in the house. But tonight, she knew that sleep wasn't going to come. Some nights were just like that, and she would study or read or watch something on TV until the sun came up and she felt tired enough to go to bed.

Maisy, her aunt's gray tiger cat, rubbed up against the girl's ankle and meowed. She needed to go out. Aunt May wouldn't have a litter box in the house, so the two cats had been trained to go out in the yard. Maisy meowed again, and then was joined by the white cat, Sophie, who sat and regarded the girl impatiently.

"Alright, hold on," the girl said quietly.

Aunt May's bedroom door had been shut for more than an hour and the girl knew she'd gone to bed too drunk to be awakened easily. She tried not to make much noise anyway, as she stood up and walked through the open living room, the two cats running alongside and then ahead of her.

The living room and dining area were all of one piece, with the small kitchen off to the right. The back door lined up exactly with the front. The girl turned the cheap little doorknob lock, then opened the door just wide enough for the two cats to take their time passing through it.

The girl looked out at the dark back yard, such as it was. A space that was mostly sand, with rebellious patches of stiff grass popping up here and there. Several hundred feet across the yard was the back of a brick duplex identical to the girl's, with nothing to distinguish one yard from the other.

From where she stood, the girl could see a slice of the woods across the street to the right. There were no streetlights on the corner where her duplex sat, and the woods were just a darker mass against an already dark canvas. Streetlights were a waste of money in the public housing, she supposed. People would do what they did, dark or light, but the neighborhood really wasn't that bad.

She closed her eyes for just a moment, breathed in the crisp air and savored the sound of the wind through the leaves. Then she closed the door quietly and went back to the loveseat to see if she could find something on TV while the cats did their business.

She was flipping through the channels, hoping for an interesting documentary or good old movie in between the late night infomercials, when she heard a new sound, one so out of place and inappropriate that it made the hair stand up on her arms.

Through the open window in the dining area, over the sound of the rustling leaves, she heard footfalls on the concrete pavers leading to the back door. It was the unlikely but unmistakable sound of hard-soled shoes, moving steadily and purposefully toward the door. The door that she suddenly realized she'd neglected to lock again.

The sound was so unexpected that she froze there on the loveseat, her widening eyes fastened firmly on the flimsy little doorknob lock, the one that was pointing the wrong way to be useful.

In six seconds, everything she knew, everything she was, would be changed forever. She could do nothing for those six seconds but hold her breath and wait for them to pass.

Maggie kicked violently at the covers until her legs were free, then sat straight up in bed.

She closed her eyes as she took several deep, calming breaths. She felt a weight fall upon the mattress, heard the jangling of Coco's collar tags, and the rustling of the leaves outside her window. She'd left it open for the cool breeze and the fresh air, and she felt a chill as that breeze landed upon the skin of her neck, slightly damp from the terror of her dream.

Until last summer, she'd gone a few years without having her memories invade her sleep. She'd been free again for the last couple of months, and those months of peaceful slumber made tonight's nightmare freshly frightening.

She gave Coco a quick rub on the snout to reassure her, then slid her legs over the side of the bed. She put her elbows on her knees and her face in her hands, willing her heartbeat to slow, her breathing to be less shallow. She listened to the dry rustling of the leaves outside and realized it was fall. Overnight, it had become November. That must be why she'd had the dream.

From force of habit, she reached over and picked up her cell phone and her Glock from the nightstand, and stood up on the cool hardwood floor. It was only four a.m., but she knew she wouldn't be going back to bed.

She padded out to the living room, Coco tapping along behind her. Half-Lab and half-Catahoula Parish Leopard hound, Coco passed Maggie and ambled to the front door, then sat down and waited expectantly. Maggie unlocked and opened the door for her, watched as she made her way down the deck stairs, then closed and locked the door. She never failed to lock the door.

She walked into the small kitchen off of the living room, got a glass of water from the kitchen tap. There was a rustling noise outside the window and Maggie's lungs had already closed up by the time she saw the silhouette of her rooster, Stoopid, as he clumsily landed on the outside sill of the window above the sink. He hacked and coughed through the screen.

Maggie squashed the impulse to shoot him right off the sill for frightening her. Instead, she yanked out the sprayer and shot some cold water through the screen. He half fell, half flounced from his perch, and Maggie leaned against the counter, took another deep breath, and finished her water.

She was setting the glass in the sink when her cell phone rang. She snatched it up from the counter. She recognized Deputy Dwight Shultz's phone number.

"Hey, Dwight," she said.

"Hey, uh, Maggie," Dwight with his perpetual hesitance. "Sorry to wake you up."

"I was awake," she answered. "What's up?"

"Uh, well, Apalach PD called us out on a sexual assault over here on 12th Street," Dwight answered. Maggie could hear several male voices in the background. "The victim's aunt called PD, but the girl is asking for you."

Maggie felt a slight twinge of nausea in her stomach, and thought for a moment that she might still be dreaming.

"Who's the victim?" Maggie asked.

"Zoe Boatwright."

"I know that name," she said, thumbing through a mental Rolodex.

"African-American girl, fourteen years old," Dwight offered.

"Zoe Boatwright," Maggie repeated. "She was a shortstop when I coached the Angels."

"Okay."

"I haven't seen her in years," Maggie said. "She was in first or second grade then."

"Well, she's asking for you," Dwight said. The background noise faded somewhat. Dwight must have been moving away from the scene.

Maggie got a blurry vision of a skinny little girl with almond-shaped eyes and a gap in her big smile. The heat of rage warmed Maggie's insides and she pushed it down. An angry cop could be very effective; an enraged one was useless or worse.

"PD wants us to take it?" she asked.

"They were thinking that anyway," Dwight answered. "They're kind of covered up."

"You'll have to run it through Wyatt," Maggie said, meaning their boss, Sheriff Wyatt Hamilton.

"I, uh," Dwight started quietly, "I don't suppose he's handy?"

"Well, I don't know if he's handy or not," Maggie said a little sharply. "But I assume he's at home in bed."

"Uh, yeah. Sorry," Dwight said, and Maggie felt bad for snapping. But it bothered her that those who knew about her and Wyatt assumed they were sleeping together.

"Forget it, Dwight," she said. "I'm sorry. Do me a favor and give him a call. I'll get dressed and be over there in about twenty minutes, okay?"

"Okay, sure thing."

"What's the address?"

"Public housing. 202 12th Street, right on the corner of 2nd Avenue," Dwight answered.

"Okay. See you."

Maggie thumbed the disconnect icon, dropped the phone to the counter and blew out a breath.

She hated November.

CHAPTER

TWO

The small public housing development was just outside
of Apalach's compact downtown area. It wasn't the
historic district by any means, but neither was it par-
ticularly disreputable. The few square blocks of brick
duplexes were occupied by the working poor, black and
white, and generally well-maintained, albeit rather plain.

Zoe's house was at the back of the development, on a
corner lot. Across the street stood an expanse of woods that
remained a dark blotch against the pre-sunrise sky. Maggie parked on the street, as the gravel driveway had been
taken up by one cruiser from Apalach PD and one from the
Sheriff's Office. A paramedic unit sat in the sparse grass
of the front yard, dark and silent. Maggie could see that
the two front seats were occupied by EMT's, though she
couldn't tell who they were. She knew they were waiting
for the go-ahead to go inside and do their thing; this told
her that, outside the violence of sexual assault, Zoe probably had no other injuries. Of course, this meant little or
nothing, depending on perspective.

Maggie grabbed her cell phone and her keys and stepped out of her black Cherokee. Her hiking boots crunched through the yard and along the jagged gravel, and they and the frayed hems of her jeans were damp from the dew by the time she reached the front door.

She knocked twice, and a moment later the door was opened by Dwight. He looked more uncomfortable than usual. He didn't speak, just nodded once and stepped back to let her in. He ran his free hand through his close-ly-cropped blonde hair, and his eyes were sad. Maggie admired that about Dwight. He wore empathy on his sleeve and was neither ashamed of it nor inclined to stifle it.

As Dwight shut the door again, Maggie ran her eyes around the room. Brenda Collins from Apalach PD sat next to Zoe on the tweed couch, while Mark Sommers stood a respectful distance away, next to a cheap entertainment center. The TV was on but muted. At the back of the long room, beyond a round veneer table and six upholstered chairs on wheels, Jake Marino from the crime scene unit was dusting the outside knob of the back door. Through the open door, Maggie could see the crime scene vehicle parked just a few yards behind the house.

Standing in the kitchen doorway watching Jake, smoke from her cigarette drifting toward the open door, was a black woman about Maggie's age. There were bags under her blank eyes, and her green capris and striped top looked like they'd been slept in. Maggie had known Zoe's mom, though very casually and many years ago. But Zoe's mother had been white. She didn't recognize this woman.

Zoe's father had been Mack Boatwright, a slim, hand-some black man who had been a shrimper like Maggie's late husband. He'd been killed five years back or so, when a truck hit his car as he was driving home from Panama City. In fact, the last time Maggie had seen Zoe was at her father's funeral. Shortly after her husband's death, Zoe's mother, a quiet, pretty redhead, had moved to Port St. Joe for work and a new start.

After their rapid scan of the room's occupants, Maggie's eyes settled on Zoe.

She wasn't a small girl, though she was very slim. She looked like she might be taller than Maggie, and her legs looked incredibly long beneath her shorts and baggy tee shirt. She sat perfectly still, her spine straight as a board and her hands folded neatly in her lap. The purposeful dignity made something clench inside Maggie's chest.

Zoe had been a cute little girl, but she was an exceptionally pretty teenager. Her skin was perfectly clear, and the color of coffee with just the right amount of milk. Her long, straightened hair was up in a loose bun, but much of it had fallen or been pulled loose, and several strands hung down around her face and below her shoulders.

Zoe's large, almond-shaped eyes were focused on Maggie unblinkingly.

"Hello, Zoe," Maggie said quietly.

Zoe's voice was so low that Maggie almost couldn't hear her. "Hi, Coach," she said, and Maggie felt something inside her crumple in a heap. She kept it off her face.

"Why don't I get a rundown from Sgt. Collins before I start asking you questions?" Maggie asked. "So you don't have to repeat yourself too much."

"Okay."

Maggie looked at Brenda Collins.

"Zoe was up late, watching TV. Ms. Boatwright, her aunt, was asleep in bed. Zoe'd just let the cats out to go to the bathroom," Brenda looked down at her notepad, "at about 3:20, when a white male entered the unlocked back door. He was wearing a blue ski mask. White with brown eyes, roughly five-seven to five-ten, slim build, jeans and a dark blue tee shirt."

Maggie had been watching Zoe as Zoe stared at the coffee table, but she looked back over at Brenda when she stopped speaking. "Weapon?"

"He stopped by the kitchen and grabbed a butter knife," Brenda answered.

Maggie looked back over at Zoe. "Do you think you know him, Zoe?"

Zoe raised her eyes to Maggie's and shook her head slowly. "I don't think so," she answered flatly, her voice and face both free of emotion or expression. "Do you think I know him? Is that why he had a mask?"

"Maybe," Maggie answered. "Either he didn't want you to recognize him then or he doesn't want you to recognize him later."

Maggie turned back to Brenda. "We have a description out?"

Brenda nodded. "All available cars are looking for him. Zoe thinks he was on foot."

"He might have parked somewhere," Maggie said.

"Well, this is all we've got so far," Brenda said. "She asked for you and we decided to let you handle the rest of the questions."

Maggie nodded and pointed at the couch, wanting Brenda to make room. Instead, the other officer stood.

"I'll get us started with canvassing the neighborhood, see if any of the neighbors were up," she said. "If that works for you."

"Yes. Thank you," Maggie said as she sat.

Mark Sommers followed Brenda out the front door. Dwight held it open and looked over at Maggie. She nodded an unspoken answer to his unasked question, and he shut the door and stood back against the wall once more, staring down at the floor as though by not looking at Zoe he could be less of an eavesdropper.

"Dwight, could you take the notes, please?" Maggie asked him. He looked like he was going to say something, but then he just pulled a department tablet out of the Sheriff's Office attaché on the floor beside him. Maggie watched him for a moment as he pulled up the right screen. He glanced at Zoe almost apologetically, as though it was unkind of him to listen, then he nodded at Maggie.

Maggie glanced over her shoulder at the back of the room. Jake from the crime scene unit had moved into the kitchen. The aunt was sitting at the kitchen table now, a fresh cigarette in her hand, staring out the back window at the almost-dawn.

Maggie sat down in the vacancy that Brenda had created, and Zoe watched her impassively as she took a breath before speaking quietly.

"Okay, Zoe," Maggie started. "You were up watching TV?"

"Yes, ma'am."

"Is there some reason you were still up?"

Zoe hesitated a moment before answering. "I have insomnia sometimes," she said.

"Doesn't that interfere with school?"

"Not really. I homeschool," Zoe answered.

"Okay. You live here with your aunt?"

"Yes, ma'am."

"You and your mom?"

Maggie saw the girl's eyelids flutter almost imperceptibly. "She died last year. She had breast cancer."

Maggie felt like someone should slap her for having asked the question. "I'm sorry, Zoe," she said quietly. Maggie hadn't really known Zoe's mother except to say hello to, but she remembered a wide and ready smile.

"So you were up watching TV and you let the cats out to use the bathroom?"

Zoe nodded.

"How long after that did the man come in?"

"Maybe a couple minutes. I was trying to find something to watch for a little bit, then I was gonna try to go to bed. Then I heard him coming up the walkway."

"Where were you?"

The girl pointed at the loveseat across from them. "I was on the loveseat," she said.

Maggie looked. Pale yellow lace curtains rippled in the slight breeze coming through the jalousie windows. On one of the cushions was a small pile of spiral notebooks and books from the public library. Maggie could see that the book on top was a book of British poetry. She looked back at Zoe.

"So you heard someone coming up the back walk," Maggie said. "What did that sound like?

"What do you mean?"

"Well, he wasn't wearing sneakers if you heard him from here."

"No. No, I heard him. It was loud, hard. Like he was wearing dress shoes or something."

"Was he?"

She watched Zoe think.

"I don't think I looked at his shoes," Zoe finally said. "But he was wearing kind of scruffy jeans. And a tee shirt."

"So maybe not dress shoes, but hard soled shoes," Maggie said.

"Yeah."

"He just opened the door, or did he knock?"

"He just opened it. I didn't mean to leave it unlocked," she said almost defensively.

Maggie covered one of the girl's hands with her own. It was cold. "Zoe. Everybody forgets sometimes. No one thinks that's your fault."

Zoe swallowed, and Maggie took her hand away, afraid of imposing physical contact that might not be welcome.

"So he opened the door and walked in," Maggie continued. "Did he say anything?"

"He told me not to move. Not to get up," Zoe answered. She wasn't looking at Maggie anymore, but at the window over the loveseat.

"Did he use your name? Say your name?"

Zoe thought for a moment, blinking rapidly. "No," she said to the window.

"Okay. He told you not to move," Maggie said. "Then what did he do?"

"He went in the kitchen. I could hear him rattling around. In the drawer." Zoe took in a breath. It shook and stuttered when she released it. "Then he came out with the butter knife."

"He came into the living room?"

"Yeah." Zoe glanced over to an empty space over Maggie's shoulder and pointed. "There."

"Did he say anything else?" Maggie asked.

"He asked me if anybody else was in the house," Zoe answered. Maggie saw her chest begin to rise and fall more rapidly, saw her breathing become shallower. "I said no."

She looked over at Maggie, her eyes going wider.

"I was afraid he'd go look, but I said no." Zoe let out a breath, then spoke more quietly. "I thought—I was scared that maybe he'd do something to her if he went in there."

Maggie looked over her shoulder at the aunt again. The aunt had been watching, but looked like she wanted to look away from Maggie's gaze. Maggie didn't know if that was guilt or something else, but she didn't have time to analyze it at the moment.

"You didn't have to do nothin' to look out for me," the aunt said, then took a long, nervous drag on her cigarette, the end of it flaring red. She looked away then, staring at the wall between the dining area and the kitchen. Maggie turned back around.

"He didn't see your aunt's car?" Maggie asked her.

Zoe opened her mouth to answer, but Maggie heard the aunt's husky voice behind her.

"Don't have no car," the aunt said. Maggie glanced over her shoulder at the aunt.

"What time did you go to bed, ma'am?"

"About one, I guess," the woman answered. "I was at some friends'. Got home 'bout one."

The aunt spoke to Maggie, but stared at the wall in front of her, dragging hard on her cigarette. Maggie was trying not to dislike her, but something told her she would anyway.

"Did you see anyone around when you came home?' she asked her.

The woman shook her head slowly. "No. Didn't see anyone around."

Maggie turned back to Zoe. "What about you, Zoe? Did you see anyone hanging around last night, even early in the night?"

"No, ma'am."

"Any neighbors paying attention to you, or strangers in the neighborhood that you've noticed?"

Zoe shook her head.

"Okay, so you told him no one else was in the house. Then what happened?"

"He said to come here, and I got up. I thought I was gonna fall down. My legs were shaking."

Maggie nodded at her, and waited for her to continue. Zoe stared at the space where someone had reordered her world just a couple of hours earlier.

"I went over there, and he told me to lie down on the floor. He said to get down," Zoe said.

Maggie saw the girl's hands begin to tremble, though they were still folded neatly in her lap. She resisted the strong pull to take those hands.

"So you did what he said," Maggie prompted.

"No!" The word was quiet, though it seemed to leap from her mouth, almost as though the answer surprised even her. She looked at Maggie. "I was—I thought we might make noise, that I would scream or something, and I was scared she'd wake up and come out and he'd do something."

Zoe cut her eyes nervously toward her aunt, and Maggie leaned just a hair, forced her to focus on Maggie's face.

"So what did you do?" she asked softly.

"I said I didn't want it to happen here, that I didn't want something bad to happen in my house, and I asked him if we could go outside."

"Okay."

Zoe took a deep, shaky breath and let it out before she went on. "Um, he thought about that for a minute, then he grabbed my elbow and took me out back, out the back door."

Maggie watched Zoe's left hand rub at her right elbow, though Zoe herself didn't seem to notice.

"So, we went out the back door, and he was looking around, then he pointed over at the woods and he told me to go on."

The woods. Maggie swallowed and tried not to distract herself with herself. It wasn't the same. Yes, it was November, but it wasn't Thanksgiving weekend. Zoe was fourteen, not fifteen. And Maggie hadn't been taken to the woods; she'd already been there, fishing. It was uncomfortably similar, but it wasn't the same. Maggie blinked the thoughts away and focused on the graceful curve of Zoe's jaw.

"Can you show me where?" she asked.

"Show you?"

"We don't have to go over there," Maggie said. "Can you just point out the back door and show me where?

Zoe nodded. Maggie stood up and held out a hand, and Zoe took it and got up from the couch. Maggie could see her knees shaking, from fear, the aftereffects of adrenaline, or both.

Maggie led the girl to the back door, not looking at the aunt when the woman pulled her feet out of the way.

Once they were standing in the open doorway, Maggie waited while Zoe looked at the woods across the street. Her full lower lip began to tremble, and after a moment, she lifted a shaking hand and pointed.

"Where that big old tree is, by the telephone pole. There's a path there. You can't see it right now because it's dark, but there's a path there. Kids go in there and smoke weed or drink beer."

Maggie nodded. "How far in did you go?"

Zoe looked at her, looking paler than she had been, and thought a moment. "Not far. Like maybe ten feet? It was by a tire. There's an old tire back there."

"Okay. Did he leave you there afterwards?"

"No, he walked me back here, to the door, and told me to go inside."

"Did you see him leave?"

"No, he closed the door. But I heard him go that way," Zoe said, pointing through the back yards toward Bluff Road.

"Okay. That's fine for now," Maggie said. "Let's go sit back down."

On the way back into the living room, Maggie looked over at Dwight. "Would you go ask somebody to go over there and tape off a perimeter? Tell them to make it wide and stay there. I'll be out there in a little bit."

Dwight nodded and went out the front door. Maggie walked Zoe back to the couch and then waited for Dwight to return before she led Zoe carefully, patiently, through the rest of the details. Dwight tapped his notes out rapidly. The aunt never said another word; the only thing Maggie heard from her was the frequent rasp of her lighter as she sparked up another cigarette.

THREE

B y the time Maggie had taken Zoe through what would be only the first run-through of the attack, the sun had risen and the neighborhood was fully awake.

Maggie let the paramedics in to check Zoe's vitals and other measures of wellbeing, or the lack of it, and she walked through the back door and across the street. A few people stood on their patios or in their doorways, watching her make her way to the woods. Maggie felt badly for Zoe. In a town with just over two thousand people in it, it really didn't matter that Zoe's name wouldn't be released to the paper. Everyone would eventually know anyway.

Mark Sommers had pulled his Apalach PD cruiser around to the woods, and was leaning against the driver's side door. He stood and nodded at Maggie as she approached.

"I'm just gonna take a look," she said to him, her hiking boots crunching through the gravel that edged the road. "I'll let Jake handle the scene."

"Gotcha," Mark said, and Maggie hunched under the crime scene tape at the start of the footpath that led into the woods.

Maggie walked alongside the path rather than directly on it, although there was so much gravel and sand that shoe prints were extremely unlikely. She had only gone a few yards when she reached a small clearing surrounded by crime scene tape on stakes. When she looked back toward the road, she could barely see it through the trees. This spot would have been private enough.

An old truck tire filled with trash sat in the center of the clearing. There were soda and beer cans, bent and crumpled cigarette packs and candy wrappers in and around the tire, decorated nicely with an abundance of cigarette butts in various stages of decomposition.

Most of the trash was faded and water-damaged enough to be identified as old, but it was clear that some of the items were of more recent vintage. This wasn't a nightly hangout, but it was well-used. It would be hard to know what should be collected and what shouldn't, so Maggie would have them take everything.

Maggie continued around the perimeter to the other side of the clearing. Something metallic flashed at her from a patch of grass, and she carefully stepped over the tape to get a better look. When she bent over, she saw it was a butter knife, damp with dew.

Zoe had said that he'd never actually threatened her with the knife, and she couldn't remember seeing it once they'd gotten to the woods. Maggie understood very well that Zoe's mind had been working at three times its normal velocity, trying to take in or discard so many thoughts simultaneously. Details got lost. Sometimes this was a blessing.

When Maggie stepped out of the woods onto the road, she saw Wyatt getting ready to cross the street from Zoe's back yard.

Wyatt Hamilton was her boss, the Sheriff of Franklin County, for a couple more weeks, anyway. His Sheriff's Office cap was pulled low over his brow, his brown hair peeping out around the edges. At six-four, he was more than a foot taller than Maggie; his legs reaching to her stomach.

Wyatt was wearing a tee shirt and jeans, but had thrown on a navy department windbreaker, either to look more official on his day off, or to ward off the slight morning chill. Close to fifty, he was as lean and hard as any of the younger men in the department, and easily the best-looking man Maggie had ever met.

As Maggie met him in the middle of the street, she got a faint, familiar whiff of Nautilus. She would have smiled, but she wasn't feeling smiley. Apparently, neither was Wyatt; his mouth was set in a grimace beneath his thick moustache and there was no sign of his usually disarming dimples.

He put his fists on his hips and sighed. "Hey," he said.

"Hey."

"Anything?"

"Yeah. He left the butter knife," she answered. "I'll let Jake know."

"He's taking elimination prints from the girl and her aunt," Wyatt said. "The EMTs checked her out and she's okay. As okay as we'd hope. They're ready to run her over to Weems Memorial once Jake's done."

"Okay," Maggie said. "I'll go with her."

"I figured."

Wyatt frowned down at her, his eyes concerned beneath his clenched brows. "Why don't we let Terry take this?" Lt. Terry Doyle was Maggie's counterpart. Together, they made up the entire Criminal Investigator staff.

"No," Maggie said sharply. "She called me."

"I understand that. I just think it's got potential to be upsetting."

"It's already upsetting, Wyatt," Maggie said flatly. "It's supposed to be upsetting."

"You know what I mean."

Maggie jammed her own fists onto her hips. "In my twelve years with the Sheriff's Office, I've handled nine rapes, Wyatt. And handled them well."

"How many were teenaged girls?"

"Five," she answered without having to think.

"How many were teenaged girls assaulted in the woods in November?"

Maggie was irritated, but not too irritated to be touched that he remembered what month she'd been attacked twenty-two years earlier. "None," she admitted, her tone sharp anyway. "But it doesn't make any difference."

"Sure it does," he said.

"No. The only difference is that now you know what happened to me," Maggie said. "Stop trying to protect me, Wyatt."

"No," he answered quietly.

Maggie glared up at him. He'd been her boss for almost seven years, her closest friend for two. In the last six months, they'd moved on to something else entirely. They were still figuring out how that worked.

"Are you taking me off this?" she asked him.

Wyatt took off his cap, ran his hand through his thick hair, then slapped it back on and sighed. "No. But I'm advising you that you should take *yourself* off of it," he said.

"No."

"Well, then hell." He rubbed at his moustache. "So how well do you know Zoe Boatwright?"

Maggie made a conscious effort to unwind herself, took her fists off her hips and tucked them into her jacket pockets.

"Not very well," Maggie answered. "I coached her one summer, about seven or eight years ago. The last time I saw her was at her father's funeral five years ago."

"You must have made an impression."

"I'm a female cop."

"So's Brenda," he countered. "Where's her mother?"

"She died last year. Breast cancer. I just found out."

"Crap. Poor kid." Wyatt said quietly. "She doesn't have any idea who this guy is?"

"No. That doesn't mean she doesn't know him," Maggie said. "Maybe she just doesn't know she knows him."

They started back toward the house.

"Butter knife. From her kitchen," Wyatt said. "So maybe he thinks he knows something about Florida law, but not as much as he thinks he knows."

"Yeah. Not a deadly weapon, and the fact that he didn't bring it with him means he might argue against premeditation if he ever gets to trial. But still, she's over twelve, but she's under eighteen. Won't make much difference to his sentencing."

"In any event, tells me he's probably not new to this," Wyatt said. "We need to revisit the argument against castration," he said.

"You won't get any argument from me," Maggie muttered.

"I called in a couple of our guys to help PD with the canvassing, but so far nothing."

"Anybody seen anyone new or out of place hanging out the last week or so?"

"Not that they've said."

They stopped just short of Zoe's back door. Wyatt turned to look at her. "You look like crap," he said.

"You're awesome. I just haven't had any coffee."

"Want me to grab you some, bring it to Weems?"

"It's Sunday. Café con Leche is closed and Apalachicola Coffee doesn't open until eleven," Maggie said. "There's no place to get a real coffee."

"I think I read about that in Revelation," Wyatt said. Then he opened the back door and held it for Maggie.

CHAPTER

FOUR

W eems Memorial Hospital was smaller than most
elementary schools, but it served most of Apalachicola's needs.

Located a few blocks outside of the Historic
District, on the other side of Hwy 98 or Avenue E, it was a
low-slung, one-story building that had looked quite modern when it opened in 1959. The hospital handled most of
the medical needs of the small town, had a decent emer-
gency department, and even made space for Larry Daven-
port to conduct his duties as coroner, but many residents
were sent to Tallahassee for "big" medical procedures.

Dwight followed Maggie in his cruiser, while Zoe sat up
front in the Cherokee, and the aunt sat silently in the back.
The hospital was only a few blocks from Zoe's home, but
Maggie had sensed that the aunt couldn't wait to get out of
the Jeep and light up.

She was proven right when they'd parked, and the aunt
was the first one out of the vehicle. As soon as the back
door slammed, Maggie turned to Zoe.

"You get along okay with your aunt?' she asked quietly.

Zoe looked at her a moment, then shrugged. "She's okay," Zoe answered.

Maggie decided to accept that for now. She turned in her seat so she could face Zoe.

"Okay, listen. Dr. Broderick is on today, and she's very good, very nice," Maggie said. "She's handled sexual assault cases before."

"Okay," Zoe said, but she didn't look at Maggie, looked instead out the windshield.

"She's going to check you for cuts and bruises, that kind of thing, then she'll need to do a gynecological exam. She'll be looking for signs of assault and checking for DNA. Okay?"

Zoe looked down at her lap, where her hands began twisting around each other. "Okay."

"You'll be covered, and she'll get it over with as quickly as she can," Maggie said. "Your aunt can go in with you."

Zoe looked over at Maggie then, and Maggie swallowed when she saw the girl blinking tears away.

"Can you come with me instead?" Zoe asked quietly.

"Your aunt is your guardian," Maggie answered. "I can't tell her not to be in the room. But yes, I can be with you if you want."

Zoe nodded and looked back down at her hands. "Thanks, Coach."

Maggie felt her throat thickening. She glanced over her shoulder at the closed back passenger window, saw that the aunt had wandered a few yards away to a grassy median to smoke. Maggie had yet to see the woman hold or even touch her niece. The closest they'd gotten physically was in the car.

Maggie looked back at Zoe. "Zoe, why did you call me?" she asked.

Zoe glanced up at her, but then ducked her head again. "You were really nice to me when I was little. I knew you cared about me. My mom liked you a lot."

Maggie felt her throat thickening. She took a deep breath and let it out slowly before she spoke.

"I still care about you," she said. It took her a moment to speak again. "Zoe, I've been through what you're going through. Please don't be embarrassed in front of me."

Zoe looked up quickly. "It happened to you?"

Maggie nodded. "When I was fifteen."

"I'm sorry," the girl said softly, and Maggie's soul wept. "But you're okay now?"

That morning's nightmare flashed into Maggie's head. "Yes," she said anyway. "And you'll be okay, too. Different from yesterday, but okay."

⚓ ⚓ ⚓

Maggie sat next to the exam table, on the little stool with wheels, as she watched Dr. Broderick. The doctor's ash-blond ponytail hung over her shoulder as she held Zoe's right hand and gently scraped under each fingernail. Zoe sat straight as a board in her thin hospital gown, staring without expression at the wall behind Maggie.

Lynette Boatwright had quickly opted out of accompanying her niece during the examination. Her relief at having a stand-in was obvious, but Maggie didn't know if it was because it gave her the chance to take smoke breaks, or because she was uncomfortable with the proceedings. It occurred to Maggie that she just didn't care, but she tried to push that thought into a corner of her mind. It wouldn't be helpful to build a bias against the woman.

Maggie was glad that they'd gotten Valerie Broderick. Maggie didn't know her socially, but they'd crossed professional paths many times. She was in her early thirties, pretty but not in a distracting way, she knew her stuff, and she treated victims with respect.

"All right, Zoe," Dr. Broderick said gently. "I'm going to have you lie down now so that I can conduct a vaginal exam. Have you had one yet?"

"No, ma'am," Zoe answered. When she glanced at Maggie, her eyes showed her anxiety.

Dr. Broderick put a hand on Zoe's upper back. "I'm not going to start without telling you first, okay?"

Zoe nodded, just barely.

"I'm going to have to use a speculum to enable me to see any signs of injury. Do you know what a speculum is?" the doctor asked.

"Yes, ma'am."

"Then I'm going to use one of these to swab for any semen," the doctor said, holding up a long disposable swab.

Zoe nodded. Dr. Broderick moved her hand to Zoe's shoulder. "Listen to me," she said. "You didn't make an appointment for this. It's an invasion and you've already had enough invasion. I'll be as gentle and as quick as I can, all right?"

"I'm okay," Zoe said to the wall.

"Okay, let's go ahead and lie down," the doctor said gently, and she laid a folded blanket across the girl's slim hips before moving to stand at the foot of the exam table.

Maggie was surprised when Zoe reached out and took her hand. She scooted her stool closer to the table and covered their clasped hands with her free one.

"Okay, Zoe," the doctor said softly. "I'm just going to take your foot and lift it into the stirrups, okay?"

Zoe nodded sharply, staring stoically up at the ceiling.

"And now the other foot."

The reaction was so sudden that Maggie jumped just a bit. Zoe yanked her hand from Maggie's, covered her face with both hands, and let out a sob that was raw and feral. Dr. Broderick rested a hand on Zoe's knee, and Maggie let Zoe go a minute before she put a hand over Zoe's.

"Zoe, look at me," she said gently. "Look right at me."

After a moment, Zoe's cries turned to great, heaving breaths, and she took her hands from her face. Maggie gently curled her fingers into Zoe's as the girl turned her head to look at her. Maggie leaned toward her, put her face just inches from the girl's.

"Where do you look first when you stop a ball?" Maggie asked her gently.

"First base," Zoe whispered immediately.

"When can you steal?"

"When the ball leaves the pitcher's hand."

"What if you steal early?"

"Dead ball."

"Good girl," Maggie said quietly.

"Are you okay for me to begin, Zoe?" the doctor asked gently.

"Yes, ma'am," Zoe answered, still staring into Maggie's eyes.

"Who was the best base stealer on my team?" Maggie asked her.

Zoe's lower lip trembled. "Me."

"You were a fearless little thing," Maggie said quietly.

From the foot of the table, she heard the rustling of paper, and saw Zoe's eyes widen again.

"Fearless," Maggie repeated.

Fewer than thirty minutes later, Maggie had helped Zoe up and into the adjoining bathroom to change into clean sweats they'd brought from Zoe's home. She'd explained to Zoe that she'd take her home so that she and her aunt could pack a few things, then take them both to the Best Western, where Zoe could take a long, hot shower and get some rest and something to eat. Once she'd closed the bathroom door, Maggie joined Dr. Broderick out in the hallway. There were two chairs just outside the exam room door. The aunt wasn't in either one of them, but Broderick was leaning against a wall, waiting.

Maggie closed the exam room door behind her, then stood in front of the doctor, arms folded across her chest. Broderick sighed before she spoke.

"I recovered some semen. Hopefully that'll help you at some point," she said. "There was some bleeding, but that was because her hymen was intact at the time of the assault."

"Okay," Maggie said, more as a prompt than anything else. The other woman pushed some stray hair behind her ear and blinked up at the ceiling a moment. Maggie waited.

"She was full of leaves," she said finally.

"What?"

"He filled her full of leaves," Broderick said quietly.

CHAPTER

FIVE

T he Best Western Apalach Inn was located on Highway
98, about a mile outside of town, on the way to Port
St. Joe, Panama City and other points elsewhere.

Maggie checked in Zoe and Paulette Boatwright,
securing them a second floor room for the next three days.
Once the arrangements were made they went back outside
and Maggie pulled her car around to the side parking lot,
then led them up the exterior stairs to room 212.

Zoe and her aunt stepped aside as Maggie unlocked the
room, then she handed them each a key card, held the
door open for them, and watched as they took in their surroundings.

The room, with its dark-stained wooden furniture and
heavy draperies, would've looked more at home in Atlanta
or Savannah, but it was nice and it was clean. There were
two double beds, a small table and chairs, a dresser with a
flat screen TV, and a microwave oven over a mini fridge.
There was also a small writing desk next to the dresser and
it was there that Zoe placed her bookbag. Once Maggie

closed the door, Zoe looked over at her, as though looking for instruction.

"Zoe, I know you need to take a shower. Why don't you go ahead and get cleaned up and change into some clean clothes," Maggie said. "Take as much time as you need. Your aunt and I will wait here until you're ready to go."

"Yes, ma'am," Zoe said quietly. She carried her overnight bag over to the further of the two queen beds, placed it on the foot of the bed. Maggie watched as she pulled out a change of clothes and a plastic grocery bag in which she had packed her shampoo and other toiletries. Zoe moved slowly, and seemed to have to think about what to do next. After a moment's hesitation, she started toward the bathroom. She flipped a few switches in the dressing area before finding the light for the bathroom.

"Zoe?" Maggie said. Zoe glanced back over at her. "Take as much time as you need, okay?"

The girl nodded and then quietly closed the bathroom door behind her. The aunt had set her purse and her pack of cigarettes on the table, then sat down at one of the two upholstered chairs. Maggie walked over to the table and sat down in the other one.

"Ms. Boatwright, I'd like to ask you a few questions while Zoe takes her shower," she said.

"Yeah, all right," the woman said, nodding.

Maggie pulled a small spiral notebook and a pen out of her purse, then dropped the bag down on the carpet beside her.

"What time did you say you got home last night?" Maggie asked her.

"I don't know exactly," she answered. "I think it was around one."

"Is that pretty common?" Maggie asked as she jotted down her notes.

"What you mean?" Paulette asked. She didn't seem nervous about the question, perhaps just slightly resentful.

"Are you usually home in the evenings, do you go out, do you work nights?"

"I go out some," Paulette Boatwright answered. "It ain't every night, but I have a life."

"I'm not being judgmental, Ms. Boatwright.," Maggie said. "Some rapes are a matter of seized opportunity. But in a lot of cases, the victim is watched for a while before the rapist makes a move."

"I'm not a homebody," Paulette said. "I work hard. I work all day. I like to visit with my friends, sometimes we go out."

"I understand," Maggie said, as she scratched in her notebook. She looked up and Paulette held her gaze almost defensively. "This guy didn't seem to know that you were home. I'm trying to establish your normal routines. Maybe he's been watching your house, maybe he hasn't."

Maggie heard the shower turn on in the bathroom. She glanced over towards the bathroom for a moment, and remembered her first shower after she'd been attacked. The last half of it had been in cold water. Maggie's showers were still longer than most. She didn't expect Zoe out anytime soon.

She turned her attention back to Paulette. The woman was occupying her hands by tapping her cigarette pack end over end on the table. Maggie didn't know if she was nervous, or just needed to smoke already.

"How long has Zoe been living with you?" she asked her.

"Since February," the woman answered without looking up. "About a month after her mama died."

"Where was she before then?" Maggie asked.

Paulette tapped the cigarette pack on the table a few times before answering. "She stayed for a while with the lady that took care of her mama," she answered finally. "The nurse they had come in."

Maggie looked up from her pad. "Why wasn't she staying with family?" she asked politely.

"Her mom's family won't have nothing to do with her, 'cause she married a black man," Paulette answered. "I'm the only one anywhere close on our side of the family."

"So she stayed with the nurse for a while, and then she came to stay with you."

"The lady couldn't keep her anymore," Paulette answered. "One of her kids moved back home, something like that."

"How did Zoe feel about moving back here?" Maggie asked.

The other woman shrugged a little. "She didn't seem to care either way," she answered. "Long as she had her books." She looked up at Maggie quickly. "That's all legal and everything. She started homeschooling once her mama got real sick. I tried to get her to go back to school when she came here, but she wouldn't have it. I knew there was no point in trying to make her go."

"How are her grades?" Maggie asked. "Does she do well in school?"

"Girl gets straight A's," the woman answered. "She's always got her nose in those books."

Maggie tapped the end of her pen against her pad for a moment. "Do you teach her?"

"Girl, no," the woman said without humor. "I gotta work. Besides, I didn't do so well in school."

"So she studies all day while you're at work?"

"Yeah. Mostly she studies at home, sometimes she walks over to the library. She gets a lot of library books, for other stuff she wants to study."

"What about friends? Does she have many friends?"

The other woman looked up at her for a moment and looked back down at her cigarette pack. "Naw, not really. She doesn't seem to care about that." The woman flipped her cigarette pack open and closed a few times before continuing. "She went to church for little while, over there at Holiness. But she stopped after a little while."

"Okay." Maggie tapped her pen against her notepad as she thought a moment. "Have you noticed anyone that you don't know hanging around the neighborhood lately? Anyone that seems kind of out of place?"

The woman shook her head slowly. "No, not that I noticed."

"What about new service people or companies?" Maggie asked. "Maybe a new lawn guy, somebody from the cable company going door to door?"

Paulette seem to think a moment, staring at the cigarette pack in her hand. Then she shook her head.

"No, nothing like that," she said. "But I'm gone during the daytime, you know?"

Maggie nodded at her. "Okay, what about people that you've had over to the house? Friends of friends, anybody like that. Anyone seem to pay special attention to Zoe?"

"You mean people I know?" Paulette asked, her voice raised slightly. She sat up a little bit straighter. "Look, I might not be the best guardian," she said. "There's a reason I never had any kids. I'm not the mother type. I'm just trying to do what I'm supposed to do. But I don't have friends over to the house much, and when I do it's my girlfriends and so on. Men don't come to the house." She slapped at her chest for emphasis. "This ain't somebody I brought to my house."

Maggie held up a hand. "Ms. Boatwright, we have to look at anybody that could've come into contact with Zoe, no matter how they came into contact with her," she said. "It's not a judgment against you, or the people you know."

At this, the woman seem to rest back into her chair little bit, placated. Maggie chewed at the corner of her lip for a moment as she thought.

"Somebody noticed Zoe," Maggie said finally. "Somebody took notice of her, whenever, wherever, for whatever reason. It doesn't matter why. It doesn't matter what it is about her. All that matters is that he hurt her, and it's my job to stick him in jail for it."

The women stared at each other for a moment, each assessing the other. Then Paulette nodded at Maggie.

"Yeah, it is. And you do it." She flipped her cigarette pack end over end for a moment. "I might not be the nurturing type," she said. "But she's still my family, and she didn't do nothing wrong. You make sure you nail his ass."

CHAPTER
SIX

When Zoe finally came out of the shower, she was wearing baggy sweats that looked comforting, although a little too warm for the weather. Maggie took the two of them to Papa Joe's for an early lunch, avoiding much discussion and watching as Zoe quietly ate a bowl of seafood bisque. Then she took them across the John Gorrie Bridge, which crossed the bay from Apalachicola to Eastpoint, where the Sheriff's Office was located.

Maggie filed her initial report while, down the hall, Zoe worked with Jake, who used the police sketch software to come up with an image of the masked attacker that might be accurate, but would be of little help. Then she took the two Boatwright women back across the bridge, got them settled back into their room at the Best Western, and drove downtown.

She parked her Jeep in one of the diagonal parking spaces in front of the Apalachicola Coffee Company on Market Street. It was almost one, and the compact historic downtown was in full flux. The Florida Seafood Festival was the

next Friday and Saturday, and people were already starting to arrive in town.

By Thursday, pretty much every hotel room and vacation rental would be full, as thousands of people descend-
ed on Apalach to attend the state's oldest maritime festival.
Old couples, teenagers, and families with children would
spend that two days eating as much local seafood as possible, watching or participating in the oyster eating and
oyster shucking contests, enjoying the carnival rides, and
crowding around the stage for live concerts.

Maggie turned off the engine and sat in the Cherokee
for a moment. She watched a middle-aged couple in khaki shorts and bright polo shirts pause a few doors down in
front of the Old-Time Soda Fountain, waiting patiently as
their pug got a long drink from the stone dog fountain on
the brick sidewalk. It was just one of several such accom-
modations that local shop owners made for the dogs.

The bell over the door tingled as a couple in their mid-
20s came out of the Apalachicola Coffee Company, each
of them cradling a to-go cup in their hands. A few parking spaces down, two women in their 30s pulled their golf
cart in, shut it off, and walked into a tiny boutique. Traffic
downtown was rarely a nuisance. Because it was so compact, covering only three or four blocks in any direction,
most people, locals and visitors alike, preferred to walk,
ride old-fashioned pastel-colored bicycles, or tool around
on golf carts provided by local rental companies.

Maggie heard the bell over the front door of the Apalachicola Coffee Company jangle once more, and she looked
over to see the proprietor, George, standing in the open
doorway.

"You just gonna sit out there or what?" he asked her
gruffly.

Maggie got out of the Jeep and tossed him a look. "I'm coming," she said.

George turned around and walked back into the shop, leaving the door open for Maggie. She walked in and practically sucked on the air, filled with the aroma of freshly roasted coffee beans.

The Apalachicola Coffee Company was one of Maggie's favorite downtown businesses, coffee notwithstanding. With soaring ceilings and dozens of burlap coffee sacks hanging from the exposed brick walls, it was industrial chic without pretense.

The left side of the shop boasted glass ice cream freezers filled with homemade gelato, and long glass cases displaying expensive, but worthwhile, handmade chocolates. But it was the back of the shop that interested Maggie, and she walked toward the back counter, where George waited next to his elaborate espresso machine. Maggie threaded her way through a grouping of small round tables and approached the empty counter. There were just a few people sitting and enjoying their coffee or their ice cream, and Maggie was relieved that she wouldn't have to wait. Her head throbbed from a lack of caffeine, and she could feel her humanity diminishing with each un-caffeinated moment.

George, a solid, stocky man with a full head of gray hair and a consistently hangdog expression, waited for her with his palms resting on the counter.

"What'll it be, my dear?" he asked her almost wearily.

"What did you roast this morning?" she asked him.

"I got some nice Kenya, and I got Oysterman's Choice," he answered. "I'm guessing you want the Oysterman's."

"Yes, please," she answered, then her eyes narrowed slightly. "Three shots."

George sighed softly at her before answering. "You don't need three shots," he said without much enthusiasm. They'd had this conversation many times before. "This isn't Sissybucks, and the latte already comes with two shots," he said. "As you know."

"George, I'm the owner of several large-caliber weapons," Maggie said mildly.

"That's impressive," he said, in a tone that said it wasn't. "I'm the owner of this fine machine."

They stared at each other a moment, neither one of them blinking. George let out a slight sigh.

"I suppose you want it not too hot," he said.

"Yes, please."

"Because you need it now," he said.

"Yes, I do."

George stepped over to the espresso machine. "Anything else?" he asked, like he expected the answer to be negative.

"I need a latte for Sheriff Hamilton, too," she said.

He paused, a scoop of coffee beans in his hand, and looked up at her. "I suppose he wants three shots."

"Picture a giraffe on meth," Maggie said.

"Regular it is."

⚓   ⚓   ⚓

When Maggie stepped back out onto the sidewalk, a latte in each hand, she found Wyatt waiting for her.

He had parked his truck next to her Jeep, and was leaning back against his grill, arms folded across his chest. When he saw her, he pushed off and joined her on the sidewalk, his eyes focused greedily on the cups in her hand. She held his out to him and he took it from her eagerly.

"Hey," he said.

"Hey." she said back. "What time are you meeting Daddy?"

"I told him I'd be over there in a few minutes," Wyatt answered. "Want to sit a minute?"

"Sure."

They both dropped onto the bench in front of the shop, though Wyatt had to drop a significantly greater distance.

"What are you guys going out for?" Maggie asked.

Wyatt took a long swallow of his coffee and sighed appreciatively. "Gray wants to go out to St. Vincent Island for some speckled trout."

"I'm making lasagna just in case."

"Are you saying I'm not gonna catch enough for dinner?"

Maggie gave him a generic shrug.

"I'm sort of offended," he said mildly.

"Okay."

"So are we still on for dinner, then?" Wyatt asked her.

"Yeah, why not?" she answered.

It was Wyatt's turn to shrug.

"Wyatt, it's just a case," Maggie said.

"It's a rape. And you know the girl."

"I did."

"Nonetheless, I'm sure it sucks," he said.

"Every case sucks, Wyatt," Maggie said. "Maybe I should have been the one to quit the job."

"I'm not quitting," Wyatt said.

"You know what I mean."

"And what would you do? Start cashiering at the Piggly-Wiggly?"

Maggie sighed. "I don't know. But there are plenty of working women in this town who aren't cops."

"I'm happy with my decision," Wyatt said, and took a long drink of his coffee.

Maggie looked over at him. "Yeah?"

"Yes. I'm not too excited about this whole appointment thing, though."

Once Wyatt had convinced the county commissioners to allow him to make the job change, it was assumed that someone in the department would be promoted to the position of Sheriff for the two years remaining in Wyatt's tenure. However, it appeared that the governor was going to exercise his option to appoint someone.

Who that someone might be, no one yet knew, but everyone in the department was disappointed and a little nervous. The Franklin County Sheriff's office was very insular; everyone there knew everyone else and had been working together for years. The idea of someone from outside the department taking Wyatt's place was unsettling, despite the fact that he'd been an outsider, too.

"Have you heard from the commissioners yet?" Maggie asked him after a moment.

"Nope. As far as I know I've got another two weeks or so of doing my job," he said. "Then I'll be helping someone else do it."

"You know they're going to have some tough shoes to fill," Maggie said.

"I have set an intimidating standard," Wyatt agreed.

"We won't like him."

"I appreciate that."

He took another swallow of his coffee and then set the cup down between his legs. Maggie watched him out of the side of one eye as he twisted it around a few times.

"How are *you* feeling about the job change?" he asked her finally.

"Nervous."

"Why?"

Maggie took a moment before answering. "What if you decide it wasn't worth it?"

"Why would I do that?"

"I don't know," she answered, shrugging. "You could find out I'm less appealing than you thought."

Wyatt sighed and draped an arm over her shoulders. "See, that's the benefit of being best friends for so long. I've already gotten over that."

CHAPTER
SEVEN

Maggie stopped at the stop sign in front of Zoe's duplex. The apartment was still, silent, empty. Maggie had returned the keys to Paulette Boatwright
when they left the Sheriff's office, and the crime
scene team had done and gotten all they were able to do
and get. Maggie turned left, drove along the side of the duplex, and pulled over at the spot in the woods marked by
the crime scene tape.

Her tires crunched on the gravel along the side of the
road, but once she shut off the engine and stepped out of
the Jeep, the neighborhood was surprisingly quiet. A few
houses down, some kids played on a dilapidated aluminum swing-set, but other than that, there was surprisingly
little activity for a Sunday afternoon. Maggie fiddled with
her car keys for a moment as her eyes scanned the neighborhood then came to rest on Zoe's back door. She leaned
back against her driver's door and considered Zoe's duplex.

From this spot, Zoe's back door and yard were clearly
visible, as was the window over the kitchen sink. But there
was no living room window on this side of the house, only

the two in front. Maggie chewed her lip for a moment as she thought about that. She didn't believe for a moment that this young white guy, a stranger in the neighborhood, had just happened to be walking down Zoe's street when he glanced in her front living room window and, seeing Zoe sitting there on the loveseat, then walked around to the back door to attack her.

She looked at the back door for a moment. No, he had seen Zoe let the cats out the back door. He couldn't have known whether she'd locked it or not, but for whatever reason he had decided that was his time to act.

Maggie's eyes grazed the backyard. There was a streetlamp about equidistant between the back of Zoe's house and the back of the duplex opposite her, the backyard of which blended seamlessly into the backyard of Zoe's. There was one decent-sized oak in the yard, but while it might have hidden him from anyone inside Zoe's house it would have exposed him to anyone in the house behind. If she were watching the back of Zoe's house, she wouldn't do it there.

He had been here, in the woods. Maggie looked over her shoulder across the roof of the Jeep and stared at the woods. She sighed, then pushed off from the Jeep and headed toward the crime scene tape.

Her combat boots crunched across the gravel until she threw her leg over the tape and stepped onto the dirt path.

As she made her way to the clearing, Maggie reminded herself that she had already been there that morning. True, there had been other officers around her, but being alone there really wasn't any different. This was Zoe's scene, not her own. Even so, she felt like a spider was walking up her spine. She pushed the feeling away and gave herself a mental slap.

She stepped into the small clearing. The tech guys had removed all of the trash from the center of the old tire, on the off chance that any of it might be useful. The odd soda bottle and crumpled cigarette pack had also been collected.

Maggie's boots crunched through the layer of dead leaves on the ground, and she squatted, picked up a few and stared at them.

He filled her full of leaves, Dr. Broderick had said.

A faint feeling of nausea swirled through Maggie's stomach. She stood up, took a deep, cleansing breath, and looked in the direction of Zoe's house. It was impossible to see it from where she stood, and what rapist used the neighborhood party spot as a vantage point?

She sighed, stepped over the other side of the crime scene tape, and started making her way through the woods, parallel to the road. There were a few odds and ends here and there, an old soda can, a dirty sock, a used and taped up diaper that Maggie didn't want to consider too closely.

She saw nothing warranting much attention until she had gone about twenty-five yards and come across an old oak stump. It wouldn't have been all that interesting if it wasn't at a spot almost exactly across from Zoe's apartment, about ten yards deep into the woods.

Maggie sat down on the stump and looked through the trees. If she sat up very straight, she had a pretty good view of the side and back of Zoe's duplex. She sat there for a few moments, a cold anger seeping into her chest, then stood back up. She looked around the stump for anything that might have been left behind by someone keeping a vigil of any length, but she saw nothing.

The ground was mostly gravel and leaves, with a few rebellious patches of grass taking stands that were more spiritual than literal. However, there were a few partial footprints in the small amount of dirt at hand. Maggie was better with bodies than she was with prints, but they looked like athletic shoes to her.

She squatted down and took a few pictures on her iPhone, then scrolled through her contacts for the crime scene tech number. Once she'd asked Jake to come back out and try to get the shoe prints, she pushed through the trees, too eager to get out of the woods to retrace her steps.

Once she got back out on the shoulder of the road, she felt she could breathe more easily. It was then that she noticed she was still holding one of the leaves. She tossed it down and brushed off her hands.

Wyatt had been right; it was easier for him to transfer than for her to quit. In a town of fewer than three thousand people, she lacked any marketable skill other than cop work. She also loved what she did. No, she *needed* to do what she did. But she wondered when she'd finally get tired enough of being so close to so much that was ugly.

⚓   ⚓   ⚓

Half an hour later, Maggie drove down the half-mile dirt road that cut through her five acres a few miles north of town.

The cypress stilt house her father's father had built sat in the middle of old forest that butted up to the river. Here, where the loudest sounds were the cicadas and the crickets and her chickens, Maggie felt truly herself, and truly away from the world. Out there, she was a competent cop, a modern, educated woman. Here, she was just a cracker, as her people on both sides were crackers, and she was soothed by that.

Coco tossed herself down the deck stairs with a percussion of tags and toenails, then threw herself down at Maggie's feet as soon as she got out of the Jeep. Maggie knelt down and rubbed her belly.

"Hey, baby," she said quietly, as she looked up to the deck, where Stoopid stood at the top of the stairs, emitting his usual barrage of news and interrogatory remarks. When he began to perambulate down the stairs like an old man who'd just had a hip replacement, she decided to save him the trouble, and headed for the house.

Stoopid stopped halfway down the stairs, and Maggie watched him as he pecked at his chest with a good deal of agitation, then finally flung a tiny feather over his back.

"Quit it, Stoopid," she said as she met him on the stairs, Coco trailing behind her. The rooster had been systematically plucking his chest for the last few days. She supposed she needed to run him to the vet and make sure he didn't have mites or some other chicken affliction.

Stoopid fell in behind Coco, ignored Maggie's half-hearted "not you" when she opened the screen door, and tapped on into the house.

Maggie dropped her purse on the dining room table. She could hear the sounds of a video game coming through Kyle's open door down the hall, and found her seventeen year-old daughter Skylar in the kitchen.

"Hey, baby," she said.

"Hey," Sky answered from the counter, where she was making herself a sandwich. "I got your text. I thought you were off today."

"I was. I got called in," Maggie answered.

She pilfered a slice of salami from the counter and turned to find Coco smiling up at her. Maggie tore off a small piece and handed it to her dog. Stoopid was standing in front of the fridge, trying to talk it into opening itself. Maggie gently swept him aside with her foot, took out a bowl of fruit and vegetable scraps, and then headed for the front door with Stoopid right behind her.

She dumped a handful of scraps into his cat bowl out on the deck, then let the screen door slap shut behind her as she went back inside. She put the bowl back in the fridge, and grabbed a cold RC for herself.

"You want a sandwich?" Sky asked.

"Yes, please," Maggie answered. She took a long drink of her soda, kicked her shoes out into the living/dining room, then leaned back against the small butcher block island. She stared at her daughter's back as the girl pulled down another plate and started making a second sandwich.

It always surprised her to notice that Sky was exceptionally beautiful. People said she was the image of her mother. She had Maggie's long, dark brown hair, her almost almond-shaped green eyes. The only real difference between them was Sky's cleft chin, yet Maggie dismissed her own appearance, and marveled at her daughter's.

"Dude," Sky said without turning around. "I feel your eyeballs."

"Sorry," Maggie said.

Sky turned around and brought their plates to the island.

"Has Kyle eaten?" Maggie asked.

"Little man ate a little while ago," Sky said.

She took a bite of her sandwich and watched Maggie as she chewed. Maggie took a bite of her own sandwich.

"Rough morning?" Sky asked after she'd swallowed.

Maggie sighed and put her sandwich down. "Pretty much."

Sky ate another bite of her sandwich, watching Maggie and waiting. Maggie chewed the corner of her lip and watched her back.

"You'll hear about it eventually," she said finally. "Do you remember Zoe Boatwright?"

Sky thought for a moment. "No. Wait, from softball? Like, my last year in coach pitch?"

"Yeah."

Sky put her sandwich down. "Crap, dude. What?"

"She was raped last night."

Mother and daughter stared at each other a moment.

"Here? I thought she and her mom moved away."

"She moved back a little bit ago."

Maggie watched Sky's eyes dart around the room for a minute while she assembled her thoughts.

"Is she okay?" Sky asked when she finally looked back at her mother.

Maggie shrugged. "She will be."

"Did you catch the guy?"

"Not yet."

"Did she know him?"

"I don't know. She doesn't know."

Sky picked at the crust of her sandwich without interest. "Man," she said quietly.

"Don't tell anyone, okay?" Maggie asked. "A lot of people will know eventually, anyway, but you know what I mean."

"Yeah," Sky said. She flicked some crumbs from her finger. "Man. It's bad enough her dad died, you know?"

Maggie sighed. "She lost her mom to cancer last year."

Sky looked up at her quickly, blinked a few times.

"Yeah," Maggie said quietly.

After a moment, Sky pushed her plate away.

"If you catch him, how long will he go to jail?"

Maggie shrugged. "I'm not the State's Attorney. It depends on a lot of things. But she's under eighteen, so he could get as much as thirty years, but maybe get out in ten."

"Can we kill him when he gets out?"

Maggie tried for a smile, almost managed it. "Why not? We'll make a family outing of it."

M aggie stepped over to the 1940s porcelain farm sink beneath the kitchen window. It had been salvaged from her grandmother's house in 1972 after Hurricane Agnes, and it was Maggie's favorite thing in the house. If the house ever burned, Maggie would get the kids and dog out, then likely die trying to rip out the sink.

She ran hot water into the left side of the sink, squirted in some dish soap, and watched as the steam floated up, then was gently scattered by the breeze coming through the screen. The air coming into the kitchen tasted of brine and mulch and mud. It was full dark outside, and the woods were loud. The cicadas had given way to the crickets and frogs, and the leaves of the old growth oaks rattled and rustled along with them.

Maggie heard the screen door scrape open and slap shut as she slid the plates into the soapy water. She looked over her shoulder as Wyatt and Kyle walked into the kitchen.

"Your henfolk are in their coop for the night," Wyatt said.

"Did you get Stoopid to go in there?" Maggie asked.

"Please," Kyle said, grabbing a bottle of water from the fridge.

"He walked out there with us," Wyatt answered as he came to stand beside her at the sink. Maggie's kitchen was already fairly small, but it always shrank whenever Wyatt entered.

"Where is he?"

"Waiting for somebody to turn on the TV," Kyle said.

Maggie sighed and dropped a clean plate into the other side of the sink. "We might have to eat him," she said.

"That's convincing," Wyatt said.

Kyle came up behind Maggie and gave her a one-armed hug. "Night, Mom," he said.

Maggie dropped the plate she was washing back into the water, wiped her hands on her jeans, and turned to wrap her arms around his shoulders. "Night, buddy," she said, then kissed the top of his head, taking a moment to inhale his scent of Herbal Essence, sun, and boy. "See you in the morning."

"Night, Wyatt," Kyle said as he headed out of the kitchen.

"See ya, Kyle."

Wyatt pulled a dish towel from its hook and started drying one of the clean plates. Maggie looked up at his profile for a moment, at the deep dimples alongside his mouth, the strong chin, the eyebrows pulled together in thought.

"Do I have a booger?" he asked her without looking up.

Maggie smiled. "Can't I just stare at you?"

"I'm kinda getting to you, huh?" he asked, trying not to smile.

"Always," Maggie said.

He finished drying the plate and set it in the open cupboard that was a stretch for Maggie but barely above his eye level. He picked up another plate.

"I am tantalizing," he said. "But what's on your mind?"

Maggie sighed, then starting washing again. "You could change your mind," she said. "About stepping down."

It was a moment before Wyatt answered. "I probably couldn't," he said. "But I wouldn't anyway."

"You love being the sheriff. And you're the best one we've had in years. I just want it to be good enough for you," she said. "You know, the reason that you're doing it."

"It will be," Wyatt said. "We've been friends, good friends, long enough to know what bugs us about each other, and what we depend on." He looked at her as he held out a hand for another plate. "It doesn't have to be perfect to be worth it, Maggie. It won't be perfect."

Maggie tried for a laugh, but didn't quite bring it to pass. "No, it won't be that."

"We have some things to work through, but we'll do that."

Maggie finished washing the plate in her hands, distracting herself with the heat of the water.

"Boudreaux," she said quietly.

"That," he said.

They worked in silence for a moment.

"I know it's hard for you to get," she said finally.

After a moment, he put another plate on the shelf, then put the dish towel down and turned to look at her.

"It's really not," he said. "I'm a guy, and even I can see the appeal. He's smooth as satin, he's better looking than most men half his age, he's downright courtly, for crying out loud, and he saved your damn life. What's not to like?"

"It's not sexual, Wyatt," Maggie said with some urgency.

"If I thought it was, I'd be drying somebody else's dishes, Maggie."

She turned to look at him, a pinprick of panic in her chest.

"Let me clarify that," Wyatt said. "I believe it's not sexual for *you.*"

"Or him," she said.

"I think you might be wrong about that, but we've hashed over that before," Wyatt said. "Look, it doesn't even matter why he's become so…involved with you. It's about who he is. Yeah, he killed a guy, and almost got killed, saving your life. If I had been the one to come through your door at that moment, Alessi would be just as dead. I don't fault Boudreaux for that. But don't forget that he also chopped a guy up and threw him in the Gulf just for watching you get raped twenty years ago. It takes a certain kind of guy to chop a person up, Maggie."

Maggie had stopped even pretending to wash the plate in front of her. She stared into the sink as little bubbles of dish soap burst on the surface of the water. The way Boudreaux had disposed of Sport Wilmette still got to her. When she allowed herself to think about it, it bothered her less and less. And that bothered her more and more.

She looked up at Wyatt. "Wyatt, I'll be honest with you," she said. "Everything that happened during that hurricane, what he did for me, the way we got through it together… it stays with me. It all started out as some kind of fascination, even with all of the suspicions and…concerns…but that day really just—dammit, I don't know what I want to say. It's not gratitude or debt."

"A bond," Wyatt said, surprising her. "A connection."

"Yeah," Maggie said quietly.

"Look," Wyatt said. "I get the life-and-death bonding thing. You know that. As a cop, and as a Marine. But like you said, this thing with you and Boudreaux started months before that."

Maggie nodded at him.

"Do you want to hear my theory about that?"

"I probably don't, but tell me anyway," Maggie said.

"I think that part of the reason people like us are cops is that we're attracted to the darkness in the world, in other people," Wyatt said. "We try to pretend that we get close to it because we need to understand it in order to do our jobs, but I think in some ways it fascinates us, and that scares us, so we try to stomp it out."

Maggie looked at him for a moment, grew uncomfortable with the frankness in Wyatt's eyes. "Yes, I think that's probably true to some extent," she said.

"The problem is that very few people have no redeeming qualities, no attractive characteristics at all," Wyatt said. "So, the danger in getting that close to somebody like that, especially somebody as charming as Boudreaux, is that you're close enough long enough to find too much to like about them. Then you're not just close to the dark, you're right there in it."

Maggie swallowed and stared at a chip in the porcelain sink. It took a long moment for her to answer. "Are you telling me that I have to choose?" she asked quietly.

Wyatt didn't look at her, but chose to focus on drying an already dry bowl. "My dad told me once never to issue an ultimatum to someone you love unless you're ready for them to take it."

Maggie stared at him. She could tell by the set of his shoulders, by the tightness in his jaw, that he felt it. He didn't look at her when he finally spoke.

"If I'd known I was going to say that, I would have made a big dramatic deal out of it," he said quietly. After a moment, he tossed the towel down, put a hand on the counter and let out a sigh. "But it's not like we didn't know that already, right?" he asked.

"We're not very dramatic people, anyway," Maggie said softly.

"We're really not," he agreed.

Maggie swallowed. "I love you, too, Wyatt," she said.

"I know you do," he said.

He held out an arm, and she walked into him, wrapped her arms around his waist. The small of his back was warm beneath her wet hands, and she could feel his heartbeat against her cheek. They stayed that way for some time, with nothing but the crickets and the frogs and his breath in her ear to break the silence. Then he patted her on the top of her head.

"We're going to look so silly dancing at our wedding," he said quietly.

Maggie pulled back a little. "Are you proposing to me?"

"No, little buddy, I am not," he said, releasing her. "You're going to have to propose to me. And as a gentleman, I'll have to accept."

"Me? Why?"

"Because then we'll both know you're ready, goof."

Maggie sat on the top step of the deck beside Coco as they watched Wyatt's taillights disappear down the dirt road. Once the sound of his engine had faded, there was nothing but the frogs and the breeze. All around her, the thinner branches of the Live Oaks and pines and oak trees waved like a crowd of well-wishers seeing someone off on the train. Their leaves sounded like a million pieces of paper being thrown up into the air.

The leaves bothered Maggie. He had left Zoe full of leaves, and that was something she had never encountered before. She knew it had meaning, at least to him, but she'd need help figuring out what that meaning was.

A young possum, his silver fur glinting in the moonlight, skittered down a skinny pine to Maggie's left, then trundled off toward the creek.

Maggie both loved and hated these woods. She loved them because they were her home, but sometimes, especially on nights like this, they reminded her too much. She and Zoe had both lain on their backs in the woods, had looked up through the branches at the same sky, and been taught that everyone was vulnerable and that terrible things didn't just happen to other people.

She picked up the cell phone that sat at her feet and looked at the time. Close to eleven. She dialed anyway.

"Hello?" Zoe asked in a hushed voice.

"Hi, Zoe. It's Maggie."

"Hey, Coach."

"Did I wake you up?" Maggie asked.

"No," the girl answered. "I can't sleep,"

"Your aunt is there, right?" Maggie asked, almost afraid Zoe would say she wasn't.

"Yes. She's asleep."

"Why don't you try taking a nice, hot shower," Maggie said.

"I've had three already," Zoe said quietly.

Maggie's chest constricted, and she allowed her silence to speak on her behalf.

"I can't get him off me," Zoe said finally, her voice almost a whisper.

Maggie had a sudden vision of a tiny girl in pigtails and an oversized Braves tee shirt, softball pants cinched at the waist, lying in the dirt next to the old tire in the woods. She blinked it away.

"Maybe you should take the pill the doctor gave you," she said.

"I just did. I'm reciting 'Christabel' in my head while I'm waiting for it to start working."

"Are you lying down? You're supposed to lie down once you take it."

"Well, I'm in bed."

"What's 'Christabel'?"

"It's a poem by Samuel Taylor Coleridge," Zoe said.

"Is this for school?"

"Not officially. My online English class is a bunch of stupid stuff," Zoe answered. "But I'm studying 18th century English poetry. Coleridge is my favorite."

"Really," Maggie said. She remembered looking at the spines of Zoe's library books when the girl had unloaded her backpack at the hotel. She'd wondered at the fact that this fourteen-year-old girl was studying astronomy and the Russian Revolution on her own time. "When did you take the sleeping pill?"

"About ten minutes ago," Zoe said.

"Well, why don't you lie down and tell it to me?"

"It's long," Zoe said, with a little bit of surprise—and maybe gratitude—in her voice.

"That's okay."

Maggie heard the soft rustling of Zoe's bedcovers, then Zoe's delicate voice began to speak in a quiet, gentle rhythm. Maggie sat stone-still on the step, the breeze and the rattling leaves all around her, and Zoe's voice in her ears. After Zoe recited the first stanza, there were no leaves or old tires. There was just the sound of a child reciting by memory a poem Maggie hadn't even known existed.

Is the night chilly and dark?
The night is chilly, but not dark.

The thin gray cloud is spread on high,
It covers but not hides the sky.
The moon is behind, and at the full;
And yet she looks both small and dull.
The night is chill, the cloud is gray:
'Tis a month before the month of May,
And the Spring comes slowly up this way.

CHAPTER
NINE

The early morning sunlight streamed through the large, twelve-pane windows of Bennett Boudreaux's kitchen. Boudreaux sat at the small, round kitchen table, drinking his third cup of chicory coffee and perusing the newspaper.

Though he was sixty-two, Boudreaux could probably have passed for fifty, with his slim physique and full head of golden -brown hair, accented here and there with a bit of silver. His face had its share of lines, but starting with such a handsome base, those lines only made him look like a matured James Dean, had Dean had the opportunity to mature.

Boudreaux's Creole housekeeper and cook, Amelia, stood at the kitchen island, watching over a skillet that contained one gently sizzling egg. She and Boudreaux both looked up when the back door swung open with some velocity and an aluminum walker clattered through it, followed with lesser velocity by Miss Evangeline.

Miss Evangeline was in the neighborhood of a hundred, but didn't look a day over one hundred and twenty. Her skin was a mass of wrinkles and the color of strong tea, accented by a scattering of dark freckles and age spots. At four foot ten and less than ninety pounds, she was deceptively cute. The Coke bottle glasses, bright red bandana, and little flowered house dress only added to the illusion that she was a sweet little old lady.

Amelia set her skillet aside and crossed the room to close the door behind her mother.

"Morning, Mama," she said.

"Ain't, no," Miss Evangeline answered, making for the table.

Boudreaux stood up and pulled out Miss Evangeline's chair. "Good morning, Miss Evangeline."

"Lie to me again," she snapped. "I got the squish lizard on one my tenny ball. I tol' you long time to rid us them lizard, runnin' out in front of people like deers in the road."

Outsiders often had a hard time unraveling Miss Evangeline's odd *patois*, which was frequently difficult even for other Creoles back home, but after fifty-seven years with the woman Boudreaux had no such trouble.

He peered at the bottom of the walker, outfitted with bright green tennis balls. "What lizard?"

Miss Evangeline lifted up the feet of the walker, but only barely. "Him that's squish," she said, pointed to a small brown lizard, freshly flattened.

Boudreaux rolled his eyes as Miss Evangeline went through the protracted process of seating herself. Amelia brought a small plate over and set it at Miss Evangeline's place.

"I get you some new tennis balls, Mama," Amelia said. "You eat. Meanwhile," she said to Boudreaux, "I gon' be grateful you don't start nothin' with her this morning.' I got too much to do, me."

Boudreaux waved her off, and she walked out of the kitchen as Boudreaux took his seat. Miss Evangeline glared across the table at him as he topped off his coffee.

"What?" he asked her after he'd taken a sip.

"Them lizard," she said.

"The lizards eat the mosquitoes you asked me to get rid of," he said smoothly.

"Now you need get me some housecat for eat the lizard," she said.

"You don't like cats," he said.

"Cat don't kill himself all over my tenny ball," she said by way of rejoinder.

Boudreaux thought perhaps it might, once properly motivated by life with Miss Evangeline, but he declined to voice that opinion. He was relieved when she changed her focus to her breakfast, picking up her knife and fork and commencing to slice her egg into minute pieces.

He picked up his newspaper and had a moment of peace before she piped up again.

"Tell 'melia don't forget she pack my medicines," she said.

Boudreaux lowered the paper. "She doesn't need to pack your medicine," he said. "I told you, you're staying here."

"No, I don't, me," she said. "I go home with you."

"We went over this last night," he said. "You don't fly."

"We don't go the aeroplane," she said. "We go Mr. Benny Mercedes-Benz."

Boudreaux put the paper down and sighed. "No, we do not 'go Mr. Benny Mercedes-Benz,'" he said. "We don't have time to drive to Louisiana and back, and one of us would die on the way."

Miss Evangeline's mouth pinched up, and he could see her arranging her lower plate with her tongue. "You in the mood to run your mouth to me today, then," she said.

"We discussed this last night," he said a bit impatiently. "You're staying here. I'll speak with Maggie later today."

"I done already tol' you leave that girl alone," she said. "It ain't good for her nor you, y'all go like you do."

"And I've told you that we're going to have to disagree on that," Boudreaux said. "Now eat your breakfast."

He picked the paper back up, and heard the gentle scrape of Miss Evangeline's cutlery for a moment, then it stopped.

"Who the man on the paper?" she asked.

Boudreaux turned the paper around to see the front page, though he already knew what was on it. "Sheriff Hamilton," he answered, before straightening his paper.

"What he do?"

"He's resigning his job, taking some other job in the Sheriff's Office," he said.

"Why he quit the job?"

"According to the paper, it's because he got shot a few months ago," Boudreaux said. "But it's because he loves Maggie."

She was silent for a moment.

"Look like ever'body got the same problem," she finally said.

⚓ ⚓ ⚓

Maggie had spent all of Monday dragging Zoe through mug shots from surrounding counties, and checking the whereabouts and alibis of a few locals who had, at some point, been arrested for or convicted of sexual assaults. She'd come up with nothing worthwhile and now, sitting at her desk on Tuesday afternoon, she was feeling the pressure of time between her shoulder blades.

It was looking less and less likely that they would have this guy in custody before Zoe and her aunt went back to their home today, and she hated it for the girl. It was very rare for a rapist to return to a victim, but that wouldn't keep Zoe from expecting it every minute. In particular, every minute that she was home alone.

Maggie tapped her pen against the edge of her desk for a moment, then opened Zoe's thin case file. After a moment, she found Dwight's notes and located the name of the nurse who had taken care of Zoe before she'd sent her to live with Paulette Boatwright.

Maggie picked up her phone, hesitated long enough to decide she wasn't really overstepping her bounds, and then dialed the number.

A woman who sounded middle-aged answered on the third ring.

"Hello?"

"Hello, this is Lt. Maggie Redmond with the Franklin County Sheriff's Office," Maggie said. "Is this Gina Merritt?"

There was a moment's hesitation on the other end of the line. "Yes? Is something wrong?"

"Ma'am, I'm sorry to bother you, but I'm handling a matter that concerns Zoe Boatwright, and I just wanted to speak with you for a moment."

"I don't—" the woman started. "What about Zoe?"

"I understand that you were her mother's caregiver during her illness," Maggie said.

"Yes, just the last few months."

"You're a hospice nurse?"

"Yes," the woman answered.

"That must be very difficult work," Maggie said.

"Well, yes, but it's very rewarding," Gina said.

"I'm sure it is," Maggie said. "I understand that Zoe stayed with you for a while after her mother's death."

Gina Merritt took a moment to answer. "Yes, her mother and I had discussed it. She was estranged from her family, you know. Because of her husband."

"Yes. How long did Zoe stay with you?"

"She was here for almost three months."

"Ma'am, Zoe is in kind of a tough situation right now—"

"Is she in trouble?" Gina asked. "She's a very good girl!"

"No, ma'am, she hasn't done anything wrong," Maggie said. "But she could use a change of scenery, a little break. I haven't spoken to her or her aunt about it, but I was wondering if maybe you would be open to her visiting you for a short time?"

"Oh." The woman sounded relieved. "I'm so sorry, but I can't."

"I see," Maggie said, though she didn't. "That's all right. If you don't mind me asking, why did you decide not to keep Zoe?"

"Well, my son graduated from college, over at University of Florida, and he needed a place to stay," the woman said. "This is just a little two bedroom, you know. He slept on the couch for a couple of weeks, but it just wasn't going to work."

"I see," Maggie said. "You must be very proud of your son."

"Thank you," the woman said, and Maggie noticed she didn't agree.

"Well, I appreciate your time, ma'am, and please don't feel badly," Maggie said. "Like I said, it was just an idea, and Zoe doesn't know I'm calling you."

"Well, I do hope everything's okay," Gina said.

"Everything's fine, ma'am," Maggie said. "You have a good day."

Maggie disconnected the call and chewed at the corner of her lip, then scrolled through her contacts and dialed another number.

"Port St. Joe Police Department," a young man's voice answered. "This is Officer Landry; how can I help you?"

"Hey, this is Lt. Maggie Redmond in Franklin County," Maggie said.

"Hey, Lieutenant, what can I do for you?"

"I need to get some information on one of your locals," Maggie said.

"Hold on a sec, and I'll see who's available," the man said.

Maggie waited a moment, tapping her pen. After a moment, the line was picked up.

"This is Evan Caldwell," said a man's deep, smooth voice. "Can I help you?"

Maggie started for a moment. "Evan Caldwell? We met last month. I work for Wyatt."

"I'm sorry, who is this?"

"Maggie Redmond."

"Oh, sure," Caldwell said. "I remember."

Maggie had met Caldwell at a nursing facility outside Port St. Joe, while she and Wyatt were working on a case. Caldwell had worked with Wyatt at the Brevard County Sheriff's Office before Wyatt moved to Apalach. Wyatt had been saddened to learn that Caldwell was visiting his wife at the facility. She was only in her thirties, but had fallen into a coma after a head injury.

"I'm sorry, I'm just a little taken aback," Maggie said. "Are you working for the department now?"

"More or less. I'm sort of on loan," he answered. "I needed to keep myself busy while I'm here."

"How is your wife?"

"She's the same," he said quietly.

"I'm sorry."

"Thank you," he answered politely. "What can I do for you?"

Maggie gathered her thoughts. "I have a rape case. A fourteen year-old girl. Her mother passed away in Mexico Beach several months ago, and the girl stayed for a while with the mother's nurse. But then the nurse had the victim's aunt bring her back here."

"Okay," Caldwell said.

"The nurse says she couldn't keep Zoe because her son graduated from Gainesville and needed a place to stay," Maggie said. "I'd like to check on the son."

"Does he fit your description?"

"I don't know," Maggie said. "All we have is that he was a young white guy, slim build, about five-seven to five-nine, with brown eyes. This guy's the right age, but I don't know about anything else. I don't even know his name. I was calling about something else and I didn't want to spook her."

"Sounds like you don't have much work with," Evan said, not unkindly.

"No."

"What's the mother's name?"

"Gina Merritt. Hold on." Maggie looked back at Dwight's notes. "Lives at 434 Grant Street, in Port St. Joe."

"Kind of a trek for a sexual assault, but not unmanageable."

"No."

"Yeah, sure. Give me a little bit and I'll get back to you when I have something."

Maggie gave him her cell number, thanked him, and hung up just as Wyatt walked through her open door with an obscenely large Mountain Dew in one hand and a copy of Zoe's case file in the other.

"Hey," he said, as he folded himself into the metal chair in front of her desk.

"Hey. Guess who I just talked to over at Port St. Joe PD?"

"Who?"

"Evan Caldwell."

Wyatt's brows knit together. "What's Evan doing over there?"

"He says he's keeping busy," Maggie said.

"Huh," Wyatt said. "Did he say anything about Hannah?"

"She's the same."

Wyatt was quiet for a moment, tapped at the lid of his Mountain Dew with one finger. "So why are you talking to Port St. Joe?" he asked finally.

"The nurse," Maggie answered. "The one that Zoe stayed with when her mother died."

"Okay."

"She says she sent Zoe to live with her aunt because her son graduated college and needed to stay with her."

Wyatt opened the Mountain Dew, placed the lid on her desk. "Right age."

"Yes."

"Priors?"

"That's what Evan's going to check out," Maggie answered.

"Okay. Meanwhile, I didn't get a single hit on any cases involving... leaves. If this is a thing, it hasn't been a thing around here."

Maggie watched him as he took a long swallow of his soda. "What about any of the other details?"

"Oh, we've got roughly a million sexual assaults involving ski masks in the state this year, and so far several dozen involving an orange ski mask." Wyatt wiped at the corner of his lower lip. "Where'd this son go to college?"

"Gainesville."

"Orange and blue," Wyatt said.

"Yeah."

"Maybe we'll get lucky and he was on the UF Cross-Country Skiing team." He set his soda down on Maggie's desk and pulled a sheet of printer paper out of his case file. "How are you doing on the known scumbags list?"

"I'm about two-thirds through it. Nothing so far."

"Let's expand out of the county and add Gulf, Wakulla and Liberty counties. We can get Dwight to help us with it."

"Okay," Maggie said.

Wyatt took another drink, then studied Maggie a moment. "Have you talked to Zoe today?"

"A little while ago," Maggie answered.

"How's she holding up?"

Maggie shook her head slowly. "She's a strong girl," she said. "But she's so alone."

Wyatt dropped his chin onto his fist and looked at her hard. "Not entirely alone."

"Alone enough," Maggie countered. "I need to...I need to help her."

"You gonna rescue her, Maggie?" Wyatt asked quietly.

Maggie looked at him and shrugged, unable to either deny or defend.

"She's not Grace Cunningham," he said.

"I know."

"Your job is to catch the guy who did this to her. It's not necessarily within your power to rescue her. And you can't go back and rescue Grace."

"I know," Maggie said again. She lifted one shoulder weakly. "Maybe I'm just trying to go back and rescue myself."

"I don't doubt it," Wyatt said. "I would, if I could."

Maggie smiled at him gratefully. "I know."

They stared at each other a moment, and Wyatt was just about to say something else when Glenn Rayfield, a portly officer in his late thirties with more hair on his hands than on his scalp, walked into the office with a pink slip of paper.

"Hey, Maggie. Hey, boss," he said.

"Hey, Glenn," Wyatt said.

Glenn handed the paper to Maggie. "Some psychiatrist or psychologist or whatever called you back, but you were in the facilities."

"Thanks, Glenn," Maggie said.

"How you liking day shift, Glenn?" Wyatt asked.

"Too much light," Glenn answered gruffly, more backwoods twang in his voice than Maggie had. "On the positive side, I can go out for beers after work."

"That is a plus," Wyatt agreed.

"So when are we gonna find out who's not taking your place?"

Wyatt shrugged. "You'll know when I know."

"Everybody's pretty pissed, you know."

"I appreciate that."

Glenn looked over at Maggie. "No offense."

"Okay," she said.

Glenn looked back over at Wyatt. "I'm pretty aggravated with you myself," he said. "You've pretty much screwed us single guys who depend on our uniforms to get us dates."

"How'd I manage that?"

"Well, not that you weren't a tough act to follow already, with your damn dimples and whatnot, but then you go get shot, and then you're gonna be the damn liaison officer cause you wanna be with Maggie here?"

"I didn't get shot just to piss you off," Wyatt said.

"Whatever. All of a sudden you're the...what...George Clooney of Franklin County"

"George Clooney?" Wyatt asked, grinning.

"Whoever. Some guy that makes it so nobody else can get a date."

"When was the last time you went on a date, Glenn?"

"That's my point. Now, pretty much all I got to look forward to is gator season, since I don't feel like getting shot."

"Are you still on shift?" Wyatt asked pointedly.

"More or less," Glenn answered, and they watched him walk out of the office.

Maggie looked over at Wyatt and smiled reassuringly. "Are you embarrassed?"

"Why, because Glenn thinks I'm hot? No," Wyatt answered. "But you've turned kind of watermelon-colored."

"The inside or the outside?" Maggie asked. "Cause I feel like it could go either way."

"I feel so proud when you make an honest effort to be witty," Wyatt said. "What's with the psychiatrist?"

Maggie picked up the slip and looked at it. "A therapist I know in Panama City," she said. "I want to ask her about the leaves."

"Yeah, somebody needs to dissect this guy's crazy for us," Wyatt said, standing and stretching his back. "I'm going to go expand our sexual assaults parameters, then I'm off to physical therapy."

"When are you going to be done with that?"

"When one of us dies," Wyatt said, walking out the door.

CHAPTER

TEN

Maggie had drunk both cups of *café con leche* that she'd brought to work with her, so she was constrained to walk down the hall to the break room and pour a cup of coffee from what she considered the philistines' machine.

Once she brought it back to her desk, she picked up the message from Dr. Irene Callahan and dialed her private number.

"This is Dr. Callahan," a woman's gentle voice said after the second ring.

"Dr. Callahan, this is Maggie Redmond," Maggie said.

When the woman spoke again, there was a smile in her voice. "Hello, Maggie. How are you?"

"I'm fine, thanks," Maggie said. "How've you been?"

"Very well, thank you," Dr. Callahan answered. "I'm sorry we kept missing each other. How can I help you?"

"I'm working a rape case, and there's something here I haven't dealt with before," Maggie answered. "I'd like to ask you about it."

"Well, criminal psychology isn't really my area, but I can try," Dr. Callahan said.

"Okay. Well, when we took her for her exam, the doctor treating her found that she was full of leaves," Maggie said. "By that, I mean that he filled her...her vagina full of leaves."

The other woman was quiet for a moment. "Hm."

"Have you ever encountered anything like that?"

"Well, of course, the use of foreign objects is very common in a sexual assault," Dr. Callahan said.

"But that's not what it feels like," Maggie said.

"No. This isn't something that would signify or stand in for normal penetration," the doctor said quietly. Maggie could almost see her thinking.

"No, and the leaves didn't hurt her," Maggie said. "If he was trying to punish or hurt her, wouldn't he use something more appropriate?"

"That's what you would expect," Dr. Callahan said. She sounded distracted.

Maggie waited a moment, then grew impatient against her will. "It means something, and I feel like it doesn't have anything to do with leaves. I feel like it's about Zoe."

"Does she know her attacker?" Callahan asked.

"She's not sure, but she doesn't think so," Maggie said. "He was wearing a mask. So she might."

"If it was someone close to her, my guess would be that it was almost an apology," Callahan said. "Actually that's not the word I mean. An attempt to undo the act."

"Remorse?"

"Actually, rapists aren't known for being remorseful," Callahan said. "Rape is an act of arrogance, of entitlement. The fact that that arrogance hides a lack of self-worth doesn't really matter. So, no, I wouldn't say remorse exactly."

Maggie thought for a moment. "What about repair?"

"How do you mean?"

"She was a virgin," Maggie said.

"Really," Callahan said quietly. "Give me a moment."

Maggie chewed the corner of her lip and let the woman think a moment.

"Her virginity could have meant something to him," Callahan finally said. "Whether it surprised him or not. Yes, in a sense, he might have been trying to 'put it back,' for lack of a better term."

"Have you ever dealt with that, or heard about that motivation before?"

"Well, like I said, it's not my area. So, no, not personally, but it makes sense from a psychological standpoint."

"Okay," Maggie said, thinking.

"I don't think I've helped you much," Dr. Callahan said.

"You have. I'm just not sure how yet," Maggie said.

"Well, I have a patient due any moment, but if you need anything else, let me know," Dr. Callahan said.

"I will. Thank you."

They hung up, and Maggie sat for a few minutes, staring at the small sabal palm outside her window. Maggie felt disconnected from the world the palm inhabited. The windows in their building didn't open; the palm's fronds swayed silently in a wind that Maggie couldn't hear or feel, like a movie with the sound turned off. She was inside, where terrible things were considered and pursued, and the tree was out in the right world, the one that wasn't broken.

She tore her eyes from the window when her cell phone rang. She looked down and saw that it was Bennett Boudreaux's number.

She'd never added his name to her list of contacts, despite the fact that they'd talked on the phone several times in the five months she'd known him. It had been a conscious decision. If Wyatt had ever looked over her shoulder and asked who was calling, she would have told him without hesitation. But having his name pop up seemed like it would make her and Boudreaux's relationship more legitimate than it should be.

She was so distracted that she almost neglected to answer, and she hurriedly picked up the phone and connected before it went to voice mail.

"Hello," she said.

"Hello, Maggie," Boudreaux said smoothly, and the familiar timbre of his voice was somehow comforting. She realized that she'd missed him the last few weeks.

"Hello, Mr. Boudreaux," she answered.

"How have you been?"

"I'm fine. Thank you. How are you?"

"I'm well, thank you." He paused a moment. "I was wondering if you could stop by and see me for just a few minutes."

Maggie was slightly surprised to find that she'd really like to do that. "Today?"

"Yes. I don't want to impose, but it's something I do need to talk to you about today," he answered. "I was hoping you could come by the house."

"Okay," Maggie answered. "Well. I'm leaving the office shortly, but I do have another stop I need to make." She looked at her watch. "Would six be okay?"

"That would be fine," Boudreaux said. "I appreciate it, Maggie. I'm afraid I need to ask a favor of you."

"A favor? Is this a professional favor?"

"I hope I wouldn't ever do that,' he replied smoothly, without offense. "This is personal."

"Okay. Well, I'll be there around six," Maggie said.

"Thank you, Maggie," he said. They were both silent for a moment. "I look forward to seeing you," he said quietly.

For whatever reason, a reason she didn't take the time to identify at any rate, Maggie didn't feel right returning the sentiment. "I'll see you then," she said instead, and disconnected the call.

She sat at her desk for a moment. On the one hand, she felt a slow, shallow dread at the idea of having to tell Wyatt she was going over to Boudreaux's to possibly do him a favor. On the other hand, she had a sense of both relief and anticipation.

She sighed as she stood up, then tossed her phone into her purse, grabbed her keys and headed down the hall.

When she got to Wyatt's office, it was empty. She tapped Dwight on the shoulder as he headed past. "Hey, do you know where Wyatt is?"

"Oh, hey," Dwight said. "Yeah, he went to physical therapy, he said."

"Oh, yeah," Maggie answered. "Okay, I'm out of here. See you later, Dwight."

"See you, Maggie."

Maggie was already halfway down the hall, thankful to be able to put that one off until later. She might as well wait until she knew what Boudreaux wanted, so Wyatt could get worked up about everything at once.

Paulette answered the door of the hotel room. She was wearing lavender shorts and a tee shirt with smiley faces all over it. Maggie couldn't imagine the woman smiling, and thought someone else must have bought her the shirt.

Maggie stepped inside and let her eyes adjust to the dimness of the room. Zoe was sitting at the small round table, an open textbook and her laptop in front of her.

"Hey, Zoe," Maggie said, as Paulette shut the door.

"Hi, Coach," Zoe said quietly. There were smudges beneath her eyes, and her hair was haphazardly atop her head, held by a plastic clip.

"I just wanted to stop by for a minute and see how you're doing."

"I'm okay," the girl answered, not very convincingly.

"Do you need anything?" Maggie asked her.

Zoe seemed to think for a second, then shook her head. "I don't think so."

Maggie looked over her shoulder at the aunt. "Ms. Boatwright?"

The woman shrugged. "Vacation out of this town? I don't like makin' her go back there tomorrow."

Maggie nodded. "I'm sorry. This was all we could do. We just don't have the funds to keep you here any longer."

"I know that," Paulette said. "Just talkin'. I feel bad for her. I'd move if I could, but I don't have the money. I waited almost two years to get that place."

Maggie nodded, then looked back at Zoe. "I'm sorry, Zoe."

The girl lifted one thin shoulder. "I have to go back sometime."

Maggie swallowed, wished she had something better to offer her.

"Is anything happening?" Zoe asked her. "I mean, are you going to be able to find out who he was?"

"We're working on it really hard, Zoe," Maggie said. "I promise."

Zoe nodded. "I know."

Maggie's helplessness to give her a better answer, a safer life to return to, made her eager to leave. That made her feel like a coward. "I have to go, Zoe," she said anyway. "But if you need me, you call me. Any time, any hour. Okay?"

"Okay," Zoe said, and Maggie saw her swallow hard. She wanted to scoop her up, hold her, take her away.

"I'll walk you out," Paulette said. "I need a smoke."

Maggie followed the woman out the door. Paulette walked to the railing, pulled her cigarettes out of her shorts pocket and lit one. Maggie waited beside her, watching the sky turn darker. The cars passing by on Hwy 98 had their headlights on.

"My brother got me off of crack when I was seventeen years old," Paulette said after she'd blown out a mouthful of smoke. "Loved me off of it. Then, a little later on, I got into meth and hydros. I didn't get off them till after Mack got killed. Did it by myself."

The woman didn't seem to be asking for praise or validation; she was simply stating facts.

"That's quite an accomplishment," Maggie said. "I've heard it's a horrible process."

Paulette shrugged. "So is everything else," she said. She took another drag, blew the smoke out toward the parking lot. "I ain't no hero. I need my beer and my cigarettes. Now and then a blunt. But that's the best I can do." When she looked over at Maggie, her expression was a challenge.

"Some people would say if you can get clean, you can do anything," Maggie offered. "Maybe you're underestimating yourself."

"No, I just live in the real world," Paulette said. She turned to face Maggie, leaned against the rail. "I'm no mother. I know that. There's a reason I never wanted kids. But that don't mean I don't care about her."

"I know," Maggie said, but she felt the lie of it, knew that she did judge.

"I clean houses. I can't afford a real place, I gotta have the public housing. I know she doesn't want to go back there, but I got $72 in the bank."

Maggie didn't know what to say to that, or at least what she could say that wouldn't be empty words.

"I just want you to know that I'm not taking her back there 'cause I don't care," Paulette said. "I can't do anything else."

"Going back there will be hard," Maggie said finally. "But it'll be hard everywhere. Yes, it would be better if she never had to walk in that place again, but no matter where she is, she'll be afraid. He doesn't have to be there; he's everywhere."

Paulette watched her as she blew smoke out of the side of her mouth, away from Maggie. "You sound like you know something about that," she said.

"I do."

"They catch him?"

"He's dead," Maggie said.

"By you?"

Maggie looked out beyond the parking lot to where she knew the bay was, across the road and beyond the trees.

"No," Maggie answered. "Just dead."

M aggie sat in Boudreaux's oyster shell driveway, engine off and windows down.

The driveway was flanked by two large palms, and their fronds whispered in the evening breeze. The bougainvillea, azalea, and hibiscus bushes that surrounded Boudreaux's wraparound porch fluttered and swayed. Maggie watched them as she waited for herself not to be quite so glad to be seeing Boudreaux. After several minutes, nothing changed, so she sighed in frustration and jerked her door open.

Her hiking boots crunched through the oyster shells that made a path to the front porch of the two-story, white clapboard low-country style house. While the house was large, and considered one of the Historic District's loveliest homes, it was far less ostentatious than one might expect of the area's preeminent crime lord. As much wealth and power as Boudreaux possessed, the home was very much like the man himself: quietly, casually elegant, but unapologetic for its roots.

Boudreaux's cook and housekeeper, a Creole woman of indeterminate age, towered over Maggie when she answered the door. Her face was impassive, and she didn't wait for Maggie to explain herself.

"Mr. Bennett want you to come back to his den," she said in a deep, sandy voice.

Maggie stepped inside as the woman stood back to give her room, then closed the door. Maggie was surprised to realize that, although she'd been to Boudreaux's house several times, this was the first time she'd ever been inside.

The wide hallway was furnished with well-worn antiques that were more interesting than fancy, and the cypress plank walls were covered with photographs of shrimp boats, oyster skiffs, the Gulf, and also bayous that Maggie recognized as being in Boudreaux's home state of Louisiana.

She followed Amelia past two sets of double doors that opened off either side of the hall. One room was obviously a formal living room, and Maggie spied one end of a long dining room table within the other.

Amelia's slippers slapped against the hardwood floor as she took Maggie past a staircase, turned right into a narrower hallway, then stopped at another set of open doors.

"Maggie Redmond here," Amelia said into the room.

As Maggie stopped to stand beside Amelia, Boudreaux walked out from behind a massive antique desk. "Maggie," he said, welcome in his smooth voice. "Come in."

Maggie stepped into the room as Boudreaux made his way to her. As usual, he was dressed in casual clothes that cost more than Maggie's fancy ones would have, if she'd owned any. His khaki-colored trousers and blue cashmere pullover fit his trim frame beautifully, the sweater intensifying the startling blue of his eyes.

Two pairs of French doors on the back wall were open to the back porch, and the floor-length sheers billowed in the autumn breeze.

Boudreaux reached Maggie and held out a hand. "It's good to see you," he said, those eyes pinning her to thin air.

"It's good to see you, too," Maggie answered. She held his hand a moment, a hand that was manicured and elegant despite the callouses from a life begun in the bayous and on the oyster beds back home.

In the past few weeks, she'd forgotten how physical contact with Boudreaux always seemed to be accompanied by a slight electrical charge. She was reminded instantly, and both relieved and disappointed when he let go of her hand.

"Thank you for coming," he said.

"You're welcome."

Maggie had forgotten Amelia was standing behind her, until the woman spoke again. "Y'all want something to drink?"

"I'll get it, Amelia," Boudreaux said. "Thank you."

"Uh-huh," the woman said, and was gone.

Boudreaux walked over to a small armoire situated between the two sets of French doors. He opened it to reveal a small bar. "I'm having a glass of Moscato," he said over his shoulder. "Can I pour something for you?"

Maggie was about to say no, but remembered that he was about to ask something of her and that she was probably going to grant it. "That'll be fine. Thank you."

Boudreaux swept a hand toward a pair of cream-colored loveseats separated by a large, matching ottoman. "Please, have a seat."

Maggie sat down on the loveseat facing the open French doors. As Boudreaux poured their wine, she looked around the room. As masculine as it was, it was also quite warm.

"I just realized that this is the first time I've ever been inside your home," Maggie said, for something to say.

"It is, isn't it?" Boudreaux asked. He picked up their wine glasses and brought them over. "But the back porch really is my favorite part of the house. I can't stand being indoors."

Maggie got that. If she couldn't be on the water, she needed to at least be outside, and she spent more time on her deck than anywhere else.

She took the glass of wine that he offered, and was slightly surprised when he ignored either couch and sat down on the ottoman. His knees were just inches from hers, and she got a fleeting sniff of his understated cologne. When he looked up at her, those incredible blue eyes so close, she was reminded of the two of them, lying on a pile of debris in the hurricane, as close as they were now, both of them trying not to die. She swallowed the memory away.

"Amelia's ex-husband passed away last night. Heart failure," he said quietly.

"I'm sorry to hear that," Maggie replied, oddly surprised that Amelia had ever had a life outside of Boudreaux's home.

Boudreaux nodded his thanks, then took a sip of his wine. "The funeral is Thursday morning. Amelia's terrified of flying, and it wouldn't hurt me to attend to a few things back home in Louisiana, so I've told her I'll accompany her."

"Okay," Maggie said cautiously, then took a large swallow of her wine.

"Miss Evangeline does not fly, at all, and we don't have time to drive, even if I could withstand a road trip with her. I need to be back in time for the Seafood Festival."

Maggie waited for him to make his point, something she seldom needed to do.

 "I realize this is terribly short notice, and an imposition as well, but I was hoping you would see to Miss Evangeline while we're away," he said. "It would only be until Thursday evening. We're leaving tomorrow evening and flying back immediately after the funeral."

Maggie was taken aback by the nature of his request. She had no idea what she'd been expecting, but this wasn't it. It startled her into a moment of silence, until the humor of it hit her. It probably struck her as funnier than it deserved, coupled as it was with the relief that he wasn't asking her anything legally ambiguous.

"You want me to babysit your nanny," she said.

Boudreaux gave her half a nod and a slight shrug. "Essentially."

Maggie couldn't help smiling. "The local, uh, crime lord, is asking his friend the cop to babysit his nanny. You see the irony of this, right?"

Boudreaux allowed her a small smile. "More than you might imagine."

They looked at each other a moment, and Maggie felt a familiar pull. She'd almost forgotten the sinking sensation she always experienced when in his close proximity. It wasn't the sinking that comes with dread or regret; it was more like looking at a featherbed or a warm bath and having to choose whether to succumb. Not for the first time, Maggie declined to analyze that.

"So, what? You need me to keep her at my house?" she asked.

"No, she can't get up your stairs," Boudreaux said. "I'm afraid what I'm asking you to do is stay here overnight."

The short laugh escaped before Maggie could prevent it.

"I could get you both a room at Water Street, if you pre-fer," Boudreaux said quietly. "I'm just a little concerned about changing her environment, her routine."

Maggie sighed, then tried for a smile that didn't quite come to fruition.

"I'm sorry," Boudreaux said, his brows knitting. "I know it's a lot. But you're the only person I would trust with her."

Maggie didn't want to be flattered, or admit to it, but she was. She knew Boudreaux loved Miss Evangeline above all else.

"It's okay," Maggie said. "I'll stay here."

Boudreaux seemed just a bit surprised that he didn't need to do a little more persuading. "Thank you, Maggie."

Maggie grew a little unsettled, under the gaze of those blue eyes. She tried to distract herself from it by sighing and looking away.

"Well, this should speed up my public decline," she said with forced casualness. "Of the people who care one way or another, half think we're lovers and the other half think I've become corrupt."

"I'm sorry about your image," Boudreaux said. "I do give that some thought from time to time."

Maggie shook her head. "I'm tired of worrying about it," she said. "I've known most of these people my whole life. They'll either judge me on my character or they won't."

Boudreaux regarded her for a moment. "Are you do-ing it out of a sense of obligation or because of your rebel-lious nature?"

It took Maggie a moment to find her answer. "I'm doing it because you asked me," she finally said.

"What about Wyatt?" Boudreaux asked quietly.

Maggie swallowed hard. She hadn't had time to consid-er that factor. "I'll talk to Wyatt."

"I'm afraid he's going to dislike me quite a bit more than he already does," he said.

"You underestimate Wyatt," she said. "He already despises you pretty completely."

"That's understandable," Boudreaux said. They stared at each other for a moment. "If I were a more selfless person, I would absent myself from your life."

Maggie saw him, soaking wet and pale, slowly bleeding to death in her woods. "I've known you to be fairly selfless, Mr. Boudreaux," she said quietly.

Neither of them said anything for a moment. Maggie felt that they were each trying to see inside the other.

"Not selfless enough, apparently," Boudreaux finally said.

Maggie thought a moment about the wisdom of her question before she asked it. "Why is that, Mr. Boudreaux?"

For his part, Boudreaux seemed to consider the wisdom of his answer as well. "I would miss you," he said at last, and the frankness in his eyes was disarming.

Maggie wanted to blink, but held his gaze. "I would miss you, too," she said.

Boudreaux gave her a small smile, but he seemed to need to work for it. "My apologies," he said.

Maggie gave a shrug that looked more casual than she felt. "There's no need. I'm a grown-up."

"Would you like me to speak with Wyatt?" he asked her quietly.

Maggie shook her head and smiled without feeling it. "No, I like you both too much." She hadn't known she was going to say that, and it made her feel self-conscious. It was worse when she looked into those eyes. "Even though you like to keep secrets," Maggie said.

Boudreaux stared at her a moment, his expression unreadable. "Secrets," he said.

Maggie wanted to shut up, but didn't. "You and my father."

Three months earlier, she'd watched Boudreaux and Gray as they met for some sort of discussion out on Lafayette Pier. She'd suspected that her father was Boudreaux's alibi, or worse, in a thirty-eight year old case. When she'd gotten the courage to ask, Boudreaux had denied it. He'd refused, on the basis of honor, to explain anything else.

Boudreaux took a drink of his wine, then scratched gently at one eyebrow. "Maybe you should talk to Gray about that," he finally said.

She'd never worked up the courage to push her father for answers. If he'd lied to her, she would have known it, and that would have broken her heart.

"I suppose I will, eventually," she answered.

"Well, in the meantime, I believe Amelia has a presentation on the care and feeding of her mother," Boudreaux said as he stood and held out a hand. "We were unable to put together a documentary on such short notice."

TWELVE

When Maggie arrived at work the next morning, a *café con leche* in each hand, she headed straight for Wyatt's office. When she reached his open door, he was standing at his desk, talking on his phone. He smiled at her and held up a finger. She leaned in the door way and waited.

"What time Monday?' he asked. He waited a moment. "Okay. At the courthouse?" He grabbed a piece of scratch paper and a pen, wrote something down. "Suite 404. Okey-doke. Got it. I'll be there."

He hung up his desk phone and turned to face Maggie.

"Hey," he said.

Maggie pushed off from the doorway. "Hey," she said back.

He let out a big breath. "So, I'm going to Tallahassee Monday."

"What for?"

"Meet with the FDLE guys and your new sheriff."

"Who is it?"

"I don't know." He looked at the coffee in her hands. "Is one of those mine?"

She held one out to him. He took it, and took a long drink.

"How do you feel about it?" Maggie asked.

"The same way I felt yesterday. The same way I felt last month." Maggie stared at him, and he stared back. "It's a change. But some changes are good."

"Okay," Maggie said flatly.

"Could you at least try to look like you believe me?"

"I do. I'm just a little overwhelmed."

Wyatt sighed. "What would you do for me, Maggie?"

Maggie blinked a few times. "A lot."

"There you go," he said dismissively.

Maggie felt the pressure of guilt in her chest.

"I need to talk to you about something," she said. "You won't like it."

"What's it about?"

"I went over to Boudreaux's house last night," she said.

He looked at her a moment, his expression unreadable.

 "Why?"

"He asked me to. He needed a favor," she answered.

"Hold on," Wyatt said. He put the coffee down on his desk. "What favor?"

"His housekeeper's ex-husband died, and Boudreaux's flying with her to Louisiana for the funeral," Maggie answered. "He asked me to take care of Miss Evangeline."

"The little old lady?"

"Yes."

"Okay." Wyatt's jaw had tightened, but he kept his tone even. "Maggie, whenever your eyes start darting around my chest, I know you're about to say something I'll hate, so let's go ahead and tell and hate."

"I'm staying at Boudreaux's house."

"Hell you are," he said quietly.

"It's only for one night, and it's not like he's going to be there," Maggie said.

"I don't care if he's gone and simultaneously dead," Wyatt said. "No."

Maggie wanted to take umbrage, but even she knew she had no basis for it. Wyatt's reaction was expected and justified.

"I said 'yes'," she said quietly.

"Of course you did," Wyatt said.

He opened his mouth to speak again, but Dwight popped his head through the doorway.

"Hey, Wyatt, Burt needs—oh, hey, is this personal?"

"Beat it, Dwight, and shut the door," Wyatt said quietly.

Dwight pulled the door closed. "Go away, Burt," they heard him say in the hall.

Maggie turned back around to face Wyatt. His arms were folded across his chest.

"Evan called for you a little while ago," he said. "I took it for you."

The change of subject threw Maggie. "What?"

"The nurse's kid didn't graduate from Gainesville; he was asked to leave."

"Why?"

"A complaint of date rape," Wyatt said. "The mother convinced the girl and her parents not to press charges, but the school asked him to take off."

He reached behind him and grabbed a fax from his desk. "This is your scumbag, here."

Maggie took the fax, a copy of the kid's driver's license. His name was Stuart Martin, and he was twenty-years-old. Five-six and one hundred-thirty pounds, close enough to Zoe's description. Maggie looked at the picture. He had dirty blond hair cut in a surfer boy style, and an insolent look to his hazel eyes.

"He has hazel eyes," Maggie said.

"Hazel can look brown, especially in the dark. Especially if you're terrified," Wyatt said. "The history can't be ignored, especially since his mommy got Zoe out of the house two weeks after he got home. Maybe she saw something hinky."

"Yeah, I know. Just mentioning."

"Evan's gonna go with, since it's out of our jurisdiction and this is just a look-see."

"Okay," Maggie said again, as Wyatt walked around his desk and picked up Zoe's file. "So, let's go."

"No, you will go, and I will get out there and help Dwight look up some more of our local creeps." He handed Maggie a scrap of paper. "Go call Evan back."

Maggie stood there, feeling stupid, as she watched him head for the door.

"I thought we were working together today," she said.

"We were. We are," he answered. "But not so close together that I can reach your neck."

He opened the door and held it open for her. It took her a moment, but she finally started moving.

"You have a nice day, now," he said as she passed him.

Maggie set her coffee and purse on her desk, and dug her phone out of her purse. She stared at it for a while, trying to recover sufficiently before she had to sound normal to Evan Caldwell.

Wyatt had every right to be upset, and she knew that he did. She had also known that last night, before she gave

Boudreaux her answer. She knew he'd be angry and he was. Maybe hurt, but she hoped just angry.

Even so, it gave her a clenching sensation in her stomach to have him unhappy with her, and she took a moment to resituate herself, focus on helping Zoe, and dial the number.

"Hello?" Evan answered on the second ring.

"Hey, Evan, this is Maggie Redmond," Maggie said.

"Hey, Maggie. Wyatt give you the lowdown on your guy?"

"A little bit," she answered. "I was thinking I'd meet you at the station and we could go in one car or the other. That sound okay to you? You can fill me in on the way."

"Sounds good," he answered. "I'm finishing up some things here, but I'll be ready in about forty-five minutes if that works for you."

Maggie looked at her watch. It was a thirty minute ride to the Port St. Joe PD, more or less. "Okay, I'll be there around nine."

They said their goodbyes, and Maggie picked her purse back up and headed out.

$$\text{⚓} \quad \text{⚓} \quad \text{⚓}$$

As Maggie drove across the bridge that connected Eastpoint to Apalachicola, she composed conversations with both Wyatt and Boudreaux. She would tell Boudreaux she couldn't do it. She would tell Wyatt she wouldn't do it, and then try harder not to be so impulsive when it came to Boudreaux.

She wasn't willing—yet—to give Boudreaux up, and when she put it to herself that way, when she considered him as something to be given up, she worried about herself just a little. She had been drifting from herself since the day she'd first sat across the table from Boudreaux at Boss Oyster and found herself liking him against her will.

She was softball and Scrabble, chickens and kitchen gardens, her parents and her kids. She was Wyatt. She was not a consort of criminals, or typically drawn to things and people that weren't good for her.

She'd known Boudreaux most of her life, but superficially, first as her father's main buyer then as the Sheriff's Office's most wanted. Before June, they'd never exchanged more than ten words. How had he become so important to her in just five months? Would he have been so important if he hadn't saved her life? If she hadn't saved his?

She would have loved to talk to somebody about that, but the only person she thought she'd feel comfortable discussing it with was Boudreaux, which helped her not at all.

She drove across the bridge, through Apalach, and on to the Port St. Joe Police Department without coming up with any answers that she liked, so she put the questions out of her mind. When the Sheriff's investigator got out of her Jeep, she left the woman behind in the car. At that moment, Maggie felt the woman was too stupid to be useful.

CHAPTER

THIRTEEN

F ifteen minutes later, Maggie and Evan Caldwell walked back out to her Cherokee.

Maggie, with her long, dark hair corralled into an unenthusiastic bun and her jeans with the frayed hems, felt like a tired-looking frump compared to Evan, who looked like he'd just walked off the set of a TV cop show. His white button-down shirt was immaculate, and a green silk tie picked up the color of his eyes. He wore his shield clipped to a black leather belt holding up black trousers, and his black dress shoes were clean and polished to a shine that rivaled his almost-blue black hair.

While Evan climbed into the Jeep, Maggie checked to make sure her navy Sheriff's Office polo didn't have any coffee stains in the boob area. She started the Jeep, then tapped Gina Merritt and Stuart Martin's address into her phone's GPS before backing out.

"So, as I was saying," Evan said. "The parents have been divorced for close to fifteen years. The father's a long-distance trucker living in Kentucky. Apparently, he's doing

penance for something." He looked down at a small notepad. "No other kids."

"Any luck with the juvie record?" Maggie asked as she
pulled out onto the street.

"Not without a warrant," Evan answered. "Nobody in
the department knows the family, so no anecdotal information to share there."

"How about the mom? What do we know about her?"

Evan consulted his notes. "Fifty years old, no record
other than some unpaid parking tickets," he said. "RN
since 1986. She was a nurse at Gulf Coast Regional for several years, then moved to Port St. Joe and worked at Sa-
cred Heart until 2012. She started working for Harbor Hospice Care the same year."

Maggie turned onto Monument Avenue, and they made
their way through a working class neighborhood, the street
lined with neat but simple concrete homes in various tropical shades.

"What's the deal with the rape charge?" Maggie asked.
"How'd the mother talk this girl's family into not pressing
charges?"

"It sounds to me like the girl didn't want to press charges
in the first place," Evan answered. "The parents were trying to pressure her into it, but she did agree to bring it to
the school's attention. It would have been a hard one. She
didn't even tell the parents; her roommate did. But it was
three days after the fact."

"What happened?"

"I don't have all the details. They met at a frat party and
left together. The girl had had a couple of drinks. He was
supposed to be taking her to some club, but they ended up
at a city park. She thought maybe he'd roofied her back at
the party, because she didn't remember much about the
ride. The kid raped her in the car, then dropped her off at

her dorm because he's a gentleman. She couldn't make it to the front door, just passed out on the sidewalk, so some other students helped her in."

"Nice."

"Yeah. At any rate, the mother whined at the girl and her parents about her son's mental health issues—"

"What mental health issues?" Maggie asked.

"Depression, therapy since the age of twelve, we don't care."

"Okay," Maggie said.

"The girl and the parents agreed not to press charges as long as the kid left school and went back to therapy. He's not yet chosen to continue his career as a C student anywhere else, though the complaint is a matter of record and he probably wouldn't get accepted anywhere anyway."

"Is he back in therapy?"

"No idea," Evan answered. "He's working for a motorcycle parts place over in Panama City. Today's his day off. I asked one of the patrol cars to do a drive-by just before you got to the office. His Nova was in the driveway."

"A Nova?" Maggie asked.

"Compensating, no doubt," Evan said.

Gina Martin's home looked like most of the other homes on her small side street: neat without having much curb appeal, painted a faded light green. There were a few small hibiscus bushes near the front walk, but the grass looked wan and crispy and could use a mow. An old Buick Skylark and a primer-colored Nova sat in the driveway.

Maggie pulled in behind the Nova, and she and Evan walked to the front door.

"I'll just be window dressing," Evan said. "It's all yours, unless you need me."

"Okay," Maggie said.

Gina Merritt answered the doorbell. She was a plain woman, a good thirty pounds overweight, wearing lavender scrubs and flip flops. Maggie flashed her badge.

"Ms. Merritt? I'm Lieutenant Redmond with the Franklin County Sheriff's Office. We spoke on the phone yesterday."

The woman's facial expression changed from quizzical to worried instantly. "Yes?" She glanced over at Evan.

"This is Detective Caldwell with the Port St. Joe Police Department. He's just here as a courtesy," Maggie said. "May we come in for a few minutes?"

"What is this about?"

"We'd like to speak with you and your son for a few moments," Maggie said.

"He's asleep. What is this about?" she repeated.

"I just need to clear a few things up, get some more information," Maggie said. "We can do that now, or you and Stuart could come into the Franklin County Sheriff's Office if that would be more convenient for you."

"I don't understand. What does Stuart have to do with anything?" the woman asked, but her eyes were frightened.

"I'd prefer to discuss that inside, with both of you, ma'am, if you wouldn't mind," Maggie said, her tone almost friendly. "It'll just take a few minutes."

The woman hesitated, seemed to consider her options, then stepped back and opened the door wider for them. Evan followed Maggie into a combination living and dining room, clean and orderly, but decorated in early cat-lady. There was a glass of tea next to a small flowered recliner, and a home shopping channel was on the TV.

"I—do you want me to wake Stuart up?" the woman asked.

"Yes, thank you, ma'am," Maggie answered kindly.

The woman seemed to flutter for a moment, then picked up a remote from the arm of the recliner and muted the volume. Maggie and Evan watched her walk down a hallway, then stood there and waited, looking around the room.

There were quite a few school pictures of Stuart Martin on the wall and perched on a small bookcase in one corner, but no other artwork. A gray cat sauntered into the room and commenced to scratch at the scarred corner of a faded floral couch. Then it jumped up onto the coffee table, scattering a stack of needlework and Weight Watchers magazines.

Maggie and Evan could hear muffled voices down the hall, first Gina's, then the tenor, slightly whining tone of her son. A few moments later, Gina walked back into the room, trying not to wring her hands. She was followed by a rumpled looking Stuart, who was wearing gray sweatpants and pulling a navy tank over his head.

Stuart looked more irritated than worried, but the worry was there, too, as he looked from Evan to Maggie. Maggie got a quick up-and-down, with an extra moment spent on her chest. Evan didn't. Maggie thought about shooting him, but introduced herself instead.

"Mr. Martin, I'm Lt. Redmond from the Franklin County Sheriff's Office, and this is Detective Caldwell from Port St. Joe PD," she said.

"Yeah?"

"If we can all take a seat for just a moment, we'd just like to ask you a few questions," Maggie said.

The mother sat down hard on the couch, but the son remained standing, scratching idly at his unimpressive midriff.

"About what?" he asked.

"Zoe Boatwright," Maggie said.

"Zoe!" Gina exclaimed. "What about Zoe?"

"Yeah, what about her?"

"Could we take a seat, Mr. Martin?" Maggie asked. She gave him half a smile, but it wasn't all that warm.

"Yeah, whatever," the kid said. He sat down next to his mother. Maggie sat down in the recliner. Evan sat down in an upholstered chair next to an open sewing basket full of yarn, and leaned his elbows on his knees.

"What does Stuart have to do with Zoe?" the woman demanded, but her voice was trembling.

"I don't have nothing to do with Zoe," the kid said.

"What is going on?" his mother asked.

"Zoe was attacked in her home early Sunday morning," Maggie said.

"Man, I was right here in bed Sunday morning!" Stuart said.

"That's right," his mother said. "He came home early Saturday night, and he didn't get up until late."

"Ms. Merritt, you said you asked Zoe's aunt to take her in because the house was too small for the three of you, is that right?"

"Well, yes," the woman answered.

"Or was it because your son has had some problems with girls?' Maggie asked.

Gina just stared back at Maggie. Stuart started cracking the knuckle of one finger.

"Stuart was asked to leave the University of Florida because of a date rape complaint," Maggie continued. "Isn't that right, Stuart?"

"He was never charged by the police," the woman said, her voice an octave higher than it had been when she'd answered the door. "The girl didn't press charges. It was a misunderstanding."

"Between Stuart and the girl, or Stuart and the law?" Maggie asked.

"I didn't rape her," Stuart said, trying for a little defiance in his tone. "She came on to me at the party."

"According to our information," Evan said politely, "the girl agreed to go hang out with you. But when you took her to the park, she asked you to stop touching her and to take her to her dorm."

"That's what she says," Stuart said, his lip curling just a bit. "She was into it, man. She was just stoned and drunk."

"Stoned on what?" Maggie asked.

"How do I know? I don't do drugs, but there was all kinds of stuff at that party."

"Stuart doesn't go to parties like that anymore," his mother said.

"Stuart probably doesn't get invited very often," Maggie said quietly. Stuart looked at Maggie a little less appreciatively. "Ms. Merritt, did you ask Zoe to leave because something happened between her and your son?"

"No!" the woman answered.

"Nothing happened between me and that chick," Stuart said. "She's a kid."

Maggie didn't look at him, stayed focused on his mother. "Or because you were concerned that something might happen?" she asked her.

"No, that's not what happened," Gina said. "It just wasn't going to work out to have her here, that's all."

Maggie caught something out of the corner of her eye, and glanced over at Evan. The cat was sliding itself back and forth across Evan's ankle. Evan gently swept it aside with his foot.

"Ms. Merritt, I'm a mother. I have a daughter and a son," Maggie said. "I understand your need to protect your son. But you didn't do anyone any favors getting him out of trouble in Gainesville, not even him. I believe that you took Zoe in because you're a good person, and you cared about Zoe. Were you concerned about her being under the same roof with your son?"

"She said no," Stuart said.

"No," Gina said, but she wasn't very convincing. "I just thought it best for her to be with her aunt."

"Is she saying I did something?" Stuart said.

"No, she isn't," Maggie answered. "But you do match the general description we have. We're exploring all possibilities." She glanced over at Evan, who was carefully removing one cat hair at a time from his pants leg. She looked back over at Stuart as he piped up.

"That's bull, man," Stuart said. "I haven't seen that girl since she left here."

"You can clear this up pretty quickly, Stuart, by voluntarily allowing us to get a sample of your DNA. If you haven't done anything, then you'll appreciate being able to clear yourself of any suspicion." She pulled a small labelled packet from her purse. "I have the swab kit right here and it'll take just a few seconds."

"No way, lady," Stuart said. "I didn't do anything, and I don't have to give you no DNA."

"Maybe you should just do it, Stuart," Gina said. "Then they'll leave us alone."

"No," Stuart said. "Let her get a warrant."

"It looks better if we don't have to," Maggie said.

"I don't care what it looks like," he said.

"Stuart," Gina said.

"Ms. Merritt, maybe you could step out of the room for just a moment," Evan said politely, as he gently lifted the cat from the arm of his chair and set it on the carpet. "Some things are difficult to discuss in front of your mom."

"Why?" she asked.

"We're not here to make your son uncomfortable," Evan said kindly. "You're his mother. A woman. Just give us a few moments, please, and we'll be out of your home." He glanced at the cat as it hopped back onto the arm of his chair.

Gina thought about this for a moment, then stood.

"I don't have to talk to you anymore, man," Stuart said.

"Stuart, just cooperate with these people so they know you didn't do anything and they'll go away," Gina said. She looked at Evan as she started around the coffee table. "I'll just be on the back patio."

Maggie watched the woman go out through a set of sliding glass doors at the back of the room, then she looked back at Stuart. He'd been staring at her chest, and he met her eyes with a smirk. She was about to say something when movement from Evan caught her attention.

He dropped the cat into the sewing basket and slapped the lid shut, then stood up. "Listen up, Napoleon," he said quietly to Stuart. "Cut the swagger. Nobody's impressed."

Stuart watched Evan, wariness overshadowing the brave front, as Evan moved to stand in front of the coffee table.

"If you didn't have anything to do with Zoe, then you should be eager to cooperate with us."

"I didn't do anything and I don't have to give you none of my DNA," the kid said.

"It'll grow back," Evan said.

The kid stood up. "You don't have a warrant or anything," he said. "If I tell you to leave, you have to leave."

Maggie stood up as well. "Are you sure you don't want to help us out voluntarily, Stuart?"

"Yeah," he said, and this time he didn't look at her chest.

"That's fine, Stuart," Evan said. "But just let me mention that I've known quite a few bikers. Those old guys that hang out at your shop? A lot of them have daughters. It'll suck if they get wind of the fact that you like to roofie innocent young women."

"You can't do that, man," Stuart said. "That's libel!"

Evan looked at Maggie. "University of Google Law School," he said. He looked back at Stuart. "It's harassment, dumbass, but only when you can prove it. Don't move out of town. Go to work and come home. Run away from anyone who doesn't have a penis. This is a small town with a lot of cops who don't have anything better to do than keep an eye on you."

"That's pretty good advice, Stuart," Maggie said.

Stuart worked up a trembling sneer. "How old is *your* daughter?"

Maggie looked at him without expression until he blinked a few times, then she headed for the door.

"You're dumber than you look, which is remarkable," Evan said, then followed her out.

⚓ ⚓ ⚓

The sun blasted through Maggie's eyeballs as she and Evan walked to the Jeep.

"You don't seem to like cats," she said.

"More than I like rapists, less than I like everything else," he answered, sliding his sunglasses out of his shirt pocket.

"Maybe you should get one," she said, opening her door.

"I have one. My wife's cat, Plutes," he said as he got into the Jeep. "He's a jerk."

Maggie slid into her seat and started the car. "You have an interesting bedside manner," Maggie said.

"Entertainingly, Wyatt used to say the same thing," Evan said.

"If he's not worried about his DNA matching what we have, he's worried about it matching somewhere that nobody knows about yet," Maggie said.

"That's my assumption," Evan said.

"Mommy got Zoe out of there because she was scared," Maggie added.

Evan nodded and put on his sunglasses as Maggie backed out of the driveway. "How old *is* your daughter?' he asked her.

"Forty-five caliber," Maggie answered.

"Too old for him, then," he said.

FOURTEEN

ennett Boudreaux's rather timid receptionist had eventually said that Boudreaux had walked over to Boss Oyster for an early lunch, so that's where Wyatt went, too.

When he walked in, he saw through the wall of windows that Boudreaux was out on the back deck. He walked through the screen door, let it slap shut behind him. Boudreaux looked up, and watched without expression as Wyatt walked across the deck.

There were only two other customers outside, a pair of middle-aged shrimpers who paused in the enjoyment of their grouper sandwiches as they watched Wyatt approach Boudreaux's table.

"Hello, Mr. Boudreaux," Wyatt said. His tone was pleasant, but his eyes were hard.

"Hello, Sheriff Hamilton," Boudreaux answered. "Are you here for lunch?"

"No, I'm just here for you," Wyatt answered.

There was furtive movement across the deck, and Wyatt glanced over as the two shrimpers picked up their baskets and beers and tried to look like they weren't scurrying inside.

Boudreaux smiled. "You've frightened the clientele," he said as the screen door scraped shut. "Please, have a seat."

Wyatt sat down. Boudreaux's bottle of Red Stripe was covered with drops of condensation despite the fairly cool weather, but it was fresh enough that it hadn't left a wet ring on the table yet.

A plump young server with choppy red hair came outside, and Wyatt saw her slow her pace as her eyes darted between Boudreaux and Wyatt. Wyatt supposed it was a rather incongruous sight.

He looked up and gave her his reassuring smile, the one with all of the dimples. "Hi, Brittany."

"Hey, Sheriff," she said, brightening just a little. "Can I get you something to drink?"

"I'll have a Landshark," Wyatt answered.

"Sure thing," she answered, and headed back inside.

Wyatt and Boudreaux considered each other for a moment.

"I'm having some oysters. Would you care to join me?" Boudreaux asked.

"No, thank you," Wyatt said pleasantly. "I seldom eat phlegm."

Boudreaux gave him a small smile. "You might be in the wrong town," he said.

"Well, be that as it may," Wyatt said, and left it at that.

Brittany came back outside with a tray. She put an aluminum tray of raw oysters in front of Boudreaux, then Wyatt's beer in front of him. "You want something to eat, Sheriff? Grouper sandwich?"

"No, thanks, Brittany," he answered kindly. "Just stopped in for a minute."

She looked from one man to the other, seemed concerned with keeping them from speaking to each other. "I saw you in the paper this morning. You really gonna be the PR guy or something?"

"Something like that," he answered.

"Paper said it was because of you getting shot, but I heard it was because of Maggie Redmond. For real?"

Wyatt smiled at her. "You know how it is in a small town," he said without saying anything.

"Man, I wish somebody would quit something for me," she said as she walked away.

Wyatt looked back at Boudreaux and picked up his beer.

"I thought you weren't supposed to drink on duty," Boudreaux said.

"That's not as hard and fast as you would expect," Wyatt said after he took a drink. "Why, are you planning on bringing it up at the next County Commissioner's meeting?"

"I don't see anything wrong with a beer," Boudreaux said pleasantly.

"For the record, I don't normally drink while I'm on duty," Wyatt said. "But I'm having kind of a day."

"Have I murdered someone I don't know about?" Boudreaux asked, trying not to smile.

"I'm sure you've murdered someone *I* don't know about," Wyatt said without missing a beat.

"Not recently," Boudreaux countered. He took a drink of his Red Stripe, then set it down. "Was there something else you wanted to discuss?"

Wyatt watched as Boudreaux prepared an oyster, topping it with one drop of Tabasco and a squeeze of lemon.

"Maggie," Wyatt said. He took a drink of his beer.

Boudreaux barely looked up from his oyster. "Are you sure you won't have one?" he asked politely.

"I'm sure."

Boudreaux slid the oyster into his mouth, closing his eyes for just a moment as he bit down. Then he finished it neatly and sat back in his chair. "Maggie," he repeated.

He seemed to wait for Wyatt to be more forthcoming, and his coolness both infuriated and impressed Wyatt.

"What the hell are you doing?" Wyatt asked evenly.

"Are you talking about the favor I've asked of Maggie?" Boudreaux asked.

"I'm talking about all of it," Wyatt said. "But sure, let's start with you asking her to spend the night at your house."

"Miss Evangeline is the only mother I've ever known," Boudreaux said. "Maggie is the only person I trust to care for her."

"Maggie's a cop. You're a criminal," Wyatt said.

"That doesn't seem to have as much bearing as one would expect," Boudreaux said, then put another oyster into his mouth.

"It does from this side of the table," Wyatt said.

"Yes, I'm sure it does," Boudreaux said after he'd swallowed. "May I call you Wyatt, to save us some syllables?" Wyatt lifted his beer in assent. "Wyatt, I understand your concern. I'm not trying to damage Maggie's reputation."

"Having a slumber party at your house won't help."

Boudreaux regarded Wyatt for a moment, then sat back in his chair. "I won't be there," he said, almost kindly, Wyatt thought.

He didn't care.

"The neighbors won't know that," he said.

"I'll see that they do," Boudreaux said. "Would you like to stay there *with* her?"

"Well, not if you're not going to join us," Wyatt said.

"The offer is earnest," Boudreaux said with an appreciative half-smile.

"The offer is pointless," Wyatt said. "The two of us staying there just looks bad in a different way." He leaned forward. "What the hell is your game, Boudreaux?"

Boudreaux stared at Wyatt calmly as he picked distractedly at the Red Stripe label. "There is no game. I genuinely care about Maggie."

"Care how?"

Boudreaux gently scratched at his eyebrow for a moment. "I'm her friend."

Wyatt leaned in again and lowered his voice, despite the fact that they were alone on the deck. "*I'm* her friend. You're her job description."

Boudreaux gently slid his oysters out of the way, then put his elbows on the table and folded his hands. "Believe it or not, I have a lot of respect for you, Wyatt," he said. "I even like you, though I'm sure you'd rather I didn't. So let's not flirt with each other quite so much. Why don't you just get to your bottom line?"

Wyatt set his beer down on the table and leaned back in his chair. "My bottom line. My bottom line is this: if you do anything, anything at all, that puts her in any kind of danger, physically or emotionally, I will bury you."

"Do you mean that literally or legally?" Boudreaux asked mildly.

"Whichever way is handiest at the time," Wyatt said.

Boudreaux looked at his Red Stripe for a moment as he slowly turned it around and around. "I normally react badly to threats," he said finally. "But as a man who loves Maggie, you're well within your rights to make that one."

"I can't tell you how much I appreciate your understanding," Wyatt said without humor.

Boudreaux gently pushed his beer aside and folded his arms on the table. "But let's make sure we both know exactly where we stand."

Wyatt watched as the polite geniality slipped from Boudreaux's eyes, and was replaced with a cold intensity that a few dead men would probably recognize.

"If *you* ever hurt her," Boudreaux said quietly, "I'll scorch every square inch of earth you've ever stood on."

Wyatt smiled as though accepting a challenge, then took the last sip of his beer and set the bottle on the table. "I'd say we both know how things are," Wyatt said.

"I think so," Boudreaux said, pushing back his chair as Wyatt stood. He held out a hand. "Have a nice day, Wyatt."

Wyatt took his hand and shook it. Neither of them bothered to try for the hardest grip. "You, too, Boudreaux."

Wyatt turned and walked away, thinking that the last part there was the most believable thing Boudreaux had ever said to him. He'd have to give him that.

CHAPTER

FIFTEEN

The car was silent as Dwight drove slowly down Zoe's street. Zoe had seemed disappointed when he'd shown up at the hotel instead of Maggie, but seemed to understand when he'd explained that she was in Port St. Joe following up on a lead. The aunt hadn't seemed real happy when he said he couldn't explain what lead, but Maggie wanted to be the one to talk to them about it, and it was her call.

He pulled the cruiser into Paulette Boatwright's driveway. Both of his passengers, Paulette in the front and Zoe in the back, sat silently after he turned off the engine. Dwight looked into the rear view mirror. Zoe sat very straight and very still, staring dead ahead, until she glanced up and met his eyes in the mirror. Dwight swallowed and opened his door.

Paulette got out as well, and a moment later, Zoe got out more slowly. Paulette dug in her purse for her keys and then her cigarette case, pulled out a cigarette and lit it. Zoe stared over the roof of the car at her front door.

Paulette had her back to Dwight, blowing a plume of smoke in the direction of the woods across the street. He cleared his throat.

"Ma'am," he said quietly.

Paulette started for the door without turning to look at him, and he followed her there. As she unlocked the door, he heard Zoe's soft steps behind him.

"If you'll let me just check real quick, I'll make sure everything's okay," Dwight said.

Paulette swung the door open, and stepped aside so that Dwight could go in. He'd already been over there the day before, and he knew the techs had cleaned up any sign of fingerprint dust, but he couldn't think of anything else he could do to make Zoe feel better about walking in there.

He took a quick spin through each room. Everything was as he'd left it. He opened each closet door anyway, and left them open, so Zoe would know he'd looked. When he got back to the living room, Paulette was opening the windows to let in some fresh air. Zoe stood on the front steps.

"Uh, Miss Zoe, everything is all set in here," he said.

"Okay. Thank you," she said.

She looked up at him with those big eyes and he felt obligated, not for the first time, to tell her that there were good men. He just wasn't sure how to do that, because she wasn't asking. Instead, he stepped out of her way so that she could come inside.

Once she was inside, she didn't seem to know where to be. She looked like she was going over to the loveseat, but then seemed to change her mind a few steps in. She stood in the middle of the room, looked around, and then watched her aunt fuss over the two cats that were meowing and gliding in circles at her feet.

"I'll go get y'all's things," Dwight said, and hurried out the door.

He got the two overnight bags and Zoe's backpack—which weighed more than the other two combined—out of the trunk, then hurried back inside. The two women were right where he'd left them.

"Where do you want me to put these?"

Paulette shook her head and waved at the floor. "Just set 'em down. Everything got to be washed."

He put the bags on the carpet. "Uh, I guess I'll be getting along," he said after a moment. "Unless y'all need me to do anything."

Zoe glanced over at him, but then looked away, toward the kitchen.

"I don't guess so," Paulette answered. "We'll just wait to hear from Ms. Redmond."

"I'm sure she'll be in touch as soon as she's done over there," Dwight said. "She wanted to check in on y'all anyway."

"All right then," Paulette said.

"Miss Zoe, you take care. You can call me or the lieutenant any time if you need something."

She looked over at him. "Thank you."

Dwight nodded, then made his escape, closing the door quietly behind him. He heard someone lock it before he'd gotten off the front steps.

Zoe looked around the room after she'd locked the door. She couldn't help but look over at the loveseat, and the sense that everything about the world had changed right there gave her a twinge of vertigo. She looked away quickly, and almost started for the dining room table, but the back door was right beyond it and she wasn't ready to look at that, either.

Her aunt looked at her, the cats at her feet. "Don't have any other place to go to," Paulette said.

Zoe swallowed and nodded. "I know."

Paulette watched her for a moment. Neither one of them knew what to say for a moment. "I'll get these clothes in the wash," Paulette eventually said. "Then I guess I'll fix us some lunch."

Zoe nodded. "Okay," she said, though food made her sick.

Paulette walked into the kitchen, the cats trailing noisily behind her. Zoe grabbed her backpack and headed down the hall. As soon as she entered the hall, the air seemed to have more oxygen in it. He hadn't been there; it was still clean.

She walked into her room at the end of the hall and set her backpack on the floor at the foot of her twin bed. She looked around, and everything was exactly where she left it, but all of it looked different. The poster from her favorite movie, Franco Zefferelli's *Romeo & Juliet*. Her teddy bear, Benjamin, lying face down on top of the covers. Her papier mache mobile of the planets hanging in front of her window. All of it the same, but she was different.

She sat down on the end of the bed, stared down the hall at the living room, and waited for Aunt Paulette to call her for lunch.

⚓   ⚓   ⚓

Maggie's parents lived on Hwy 98, on a stretch just outside of town and right against the bay. It wasn't the most scenic of roads, or the fanciest of neighborhoods, but it had been affordable bayfront property back in the seventies, and it had been a great place for a water-loving child to grow up.

Maggie pulled off the highway and started down the long gravel drive. She'd picked Kyle up from school after she'd gone home and fed Coco and the chickens and packed overnight bags for Kyle and herself. She glanced over at Kyle in the passenger seat. "Do you have any homework to do?"

"Just some math," Kyle said.

"Make sure you do it, okay?"

"I will," he said. "Can't I go with you and Granddad and Sky?"

"Sorry, buddy. Granddad needs help, but I don't want to overwhelm Zoe," Maggie said. "She knows Sky, if she remembers her."

She parked next to her dad's old truck in front of the house.

"I feel bad for her," Kyle said.

Maggie sighed. "Me, too."

"I'm glad you're the one helping her."

Maggie nodded. "I hope I can."

"You will," Kyle said.

Maggie blinked a few times and then gave Kyle a smile. "You're such a good guy, Kyle.

She looked up as Gray Redmond came out through the front screen door, and she and Kyle got out as he made his way to them.

Gray Redmond was a tall, lanky man with sand-colored hair that tended to fall into his eyes when he let it go too long between cuts. He was a quiet and gentle man, a bookworm who used his words sparingly and considered them well before he spoke. Maggie watched him as he rolled up the sleeves of his old denim work shirt, revealing arms that were deceptively sinewy. There was an old saying that only an oysterman picked a fight with an oysterman, and it was true of anyone who had any sense. Decades of working those tongs had made Gray far stronger than he looked.

"Hey, Daddy," Maggie said.

"Hey there, Sunshine," he said. "Hey, buddy."

"Hey, Granddad."

Kyle reached into the back to get his backpack and overnight bag, as Gray gently grabbed Maggie's face and kissed her forehead.

"How are you, Daddy?' Maggie asked.

"I'm all right," he said. "Hey, Kyle, why don't you go on in the house and let me talk to your mother a minute? Your Grandma's got some lemon bars waiting on you."

"Okay," Kyle said. "I'll see you later, Mom."

"Hey!" she called, as Kyle started to head for the house. He stopped, walked around the front of the Jeep, and gave her a hug. "I love you," Maggie said.

"Love you, too, Mom. See you tomorrow."

Maggie and her father watched him until he reached the front door, then Gray turned to his daughter. "Where's Sky?"

"She'll be here in a minute."

"Do they know why they're spending the night?"

Maggie looked away. "I just said I was working all night," she admitted. "I'd rather lie to them than ask them to lie to Mom."

Gray tucked his hands in his front pockets and looked over Maggie's head at nothing in particular. "Your mama worries about you," he said.

"I know. But I can't really handle her panic over me staying at Boudreaux's," Maggie said. "And I can't really see her being reassured about it, either."

Gray looked down at Maggie. "Did you tell Wyatt?"

"Yes." Maggie said. She tried to crawl out from under her father's steady gaze by focusing on the keys in her hand. "He's angry with me."

"I expect so," Gray answered.

"Are you angry with me?" she asked once she got up the nerve to look at him.

Gray regarded her a moment. "No, baby. But I am worried."

"He's not going to corrupt me, Daddy."

"I'm not worried about you being corrupted, Maggie," Gray said. "I'm worried about you being confused. And I'm worried that this'll get in between you and Wyatt."

Maggie swallowed hard. "I love Wyatt, Daddy."

"I know you do."

"Maybe more than I loved David. Or differently," she said. "It's not that he's insecure about Boudreaux—"

"Aw, Maggie, don't kid yourself," Gray interrupted. "No man who's in love is secure." He looked toward the highway. "And Bennett Boudreaux is one magnetic son of a gun. But dangerous."

"He's not dangerous to me."

"There's more than one kind of danger, Maggie."

"He saved my life."

Gray nodded and looked at the ground. "That he did."

"And you're the one that sent him," Maggie said, trying not to sound as nervous as the statement made her.

"I did," Gray said. "We went over that then. I knew he hadn't evacuated."

He looked up and met her eyes, Maggie's heart rate picking up just a bit as they stared at each other a moment.

"Something you want to say, Margaret Anne?" he asked her quietly.

It took Maggie a moment to answer. "Did you and Boudreaux used to be friends, Daddy? Back before I was born?"

"No, Maggie," he said after a moment. "We were never friends."

He seemed to wait for her to ask him something else.

Were you his alibi in '77, Daddy? To her relief, she chickened out.

Gray looked up at the sound of a vehicle coming up the drive, and Maggie was grateful to see Sky approaching in her father's old Toyota truck.

"Well, Sunshine," Daddy said. "Let's get this boat in the water."

SIXTEEN

Maggie pulled into the driveway first, and Gray and Sky pulled up next to her in Gray's truck. Paulette came out of the front door and looked at Maggie curiously as Gray pulled his red toolbox out of the bed of his truck.

"Hey, Paulette," Maggie said as she walked toward the front steps.

"Hey," Paulette answered.

"I hope you don't mind, but I brought my father and my daughter over to help install some motion sensor lights for you outside."

"I don't have the money to pay for that," the woman said.

Maggie stopped at the bottom of the steps. "It's okay, these were leftovers," Maggie said, though they weren't, and she had no idea what she was saying they were left over from.

Zoe appeared behind Paulette, and Paulette got out of the way, stepped down onto the small front stoop.

"Hey, Zoe," Maggie said.

"Hey, Coach."

Maggie heard Gray and Sky's footsteps on the walkway, and glanced over her shoulder before looking back at Zoe. "Do you remember my dad?"

A faint smile appeared on the girl's face as she looked at Gray. The little girls had always loved Gray, who had helped Maggie coach the softball team for several years.

"Yes, ma'am," Zoe said. "Hey, Coach Redmond."

"Zoe. Look at you, so grown," he said with a smile.

"Hey, Zoe," Sky said from beside him.

Zoe seemed to think for a moment before remembering the older girl's name. "Hey, Sky."

"Man, you're taller than I am," Sky said, though that wasn't saying much. She and Maggie were both 5'3.

Zoe gave Sky a polite smile.

"Is it okay, Paulette?" Maggie asked.

"I guess," Paulette said, her flat tone more from embarrassment at charity than it was from apathy. "I appreciate it."

Maggie shrugged. "No problem."

Paulette stepped onto the grass and lit a cigarette.

"Do you mind if I use your restroom?" Maggie asked.

"No, go 'head," the woman answered. "Zoe, show her where it is."

"I'll be right out, Daddy," Maggie said, then she followed Zoe through the living room and down the hall. Through an open door, she could see what was obviously Zoe's room at the end of the hall. Zoe stopped just before it, next to an open door on the right.

"Here you go, Coach."

"Thank you," Maggie said.

She used the restroom, and when she stepped back out into the hall, something on her right caught her eye. Zoe was sitting at the foot of her bed. Maggie walked into the room, stood in front of the girl.

"Do they know?" Zoe asked her.

"Yes," Maggie said. "I hope that's all right."

"Do they know about you?"

"Yes."

Zoe nodded, then went quiet for a minute. "I don't feel like I belong in here anymore," she said quietly, without looking up.

Maggie sat down beside her on the bed. "Why?" she asked gently.

Zoe swallowed hard and looked around the room. "This is a kid's room," she said. "None of this stuff in here is the real world."

Maggie let out a slow breath. "That's not true, Zoe," she said. "Just because the bad stuff is real, that doesn't mean the good stuff isn't real, too."

She looked around the room, her eyes grazing the paper flowers and the stuffed animals and the stack of poetry books. "This is all still you, Zoe," she said. "This is who you are."

Zoe looked at Maggie. Her beautiful eyes looked old and tired. "I can't feel anything," she said.

Maggie took time with her answer. She knew too well that the lack of feeling was a temporary blessing. "I think that's God's way of giving your body a little time to heal before you have to heal everything else."

Zoe looked at her a moment, then looked away.

"Zoe, do you remember Gina Merritt's son, Stuart?"

Zoe looked at her quickly. "Stuart? Yes," she answered, a question in her voice.

"Do you think there's a chance that he might be the one who hurt you?" Maggie asked. She watched Zoe think about that.

"I don't think so," the girl said.

"Did he ever say or do anything that made you uncomfortable while you were there?"

Zoe shrugged a little. "He wasn't really around much.
And Miss Gina was always with us," she said. She thought
a moment more. "He looked at me sometimes, but he never said much."

Maggie nodded. "Okay," she said.

"Is that the lead you were working on?"

"Yes."

Zoe looked down at her hands, picked at a hangnail on
her thumb. "I feel like I would have known if it was him."

"Okay," Maggie said again, though she didn't think that
ruled him out.

They were silent for a moment, then Zoe looked up at
her. "I'm so tired," she said quietly.

Maggie swallowed back tears that Zoe didn't need, and
nodded her understanding. After a moment, Zoe leaned
over, cautiously, slowly, and rested her head in the crook
of Maggie's neck.

Maggie hesitated a moment, then raised a hand to the
back of the girl's head and held her. She held her for a long
while. Zoe didn't shudder, didn't cry, but hot, slow tears
crept down the side of Maggie's face and slid into Zoe's
hair.

⚓ ⚓ ⚓

Maggie left Zoe curled up asleep at the foot of her bed, and
helped Gray and Sky install motion lights near the windows and doors of the duplex, until her phone alarm went
off, alerting her that it was time to go to Boudreaux's.

She finished drilling the last bolt on a light over the
kitchen window, then climbed down off one of Daddy's

ladders. She found her father in the front, folding up his own ladder while Sky put his tools away. Maggie handed the drill to Sky.

"I gotta go, you guys," Maggie said. "Sky, you'll make sure your brother gets to school on time?"

"Yeah, I got it," Sky said.

Gray laid the ladder in the truck bed. "Hey, Sky. Run around back and unplug the extension cord for me.

"Okay," she said, then gave her mother a quick hug. "See you tomorrow, Mom."

"Bye, baby." She watched Sky walk around the corner of the house, then looked at her father. "I'll see you later, Daddy."

"Wyatt still upset?"

Maggie looked down at the gravel. "I guess. He's not returning my calls."

Gray ran a hand through his hair. "It'll be all right, Maggie."

Maggie nodded, then blew out a breath and hugged her father goodbye. "I'll see you."

Gray nodded, then watched her walk to her Jeep, pull out, and drive away.

SEVENTEEN

M aggie parked in Boudreaux's driveway next to his black Mercedes. The trunk of the car was open. She cut the engine, then checked her phone one more time to see if she'd missed a call from Wyatt. She hadn't. It was almost seven, and she hadn't heard from him since they'd left each other that morning. This alone was an unusual event. The weight of his silence pressed down on her chest.

She looked up as Boudreaux came out the front door, followed by Amelia. Boudreaux carried two overnight bags and a briefcase in his hands. Maggie got out of the Jeep and met them at the Mercedes.

"Hello, Maggie," he said.

"Mr. Boudreaux."

Amelia nodded at her. "Mama already in the bed, watchin' the television," she said. "She'll be asleep by nine, ten o' clock."

"Okay," Maggie said.

Amelia nodded again, then went and climbed in the passenger side of the car. Boudreaux closed the trunk, then looked at Maggie and ran a hand through his hair as the evening wind tossed a lock into his eyes.

"The neighbors to the left and across the street know we're going out of town overnight, and that you're watching Miss Evangeline for me," he said. "The neighbors to the right are in the Bahamas."

"Okay," Maggie said.

"I thought it best that they know I'm out of town, if they happened to see you or your car."

Maggie gave a slight shrug. "Thank you," she said. "It won't help much."

"I know."

"I don't really care," she said.

"Neither do I, except on your behalf," he answered.

Maggie nodded again.

"Please help yourself to anything you'd like to eat or drink," he said. "Amelia says there's some shrimp étouffée left from dinner."

"Thank you," Maggie said.

Those incredible blue eyes drilled into her own, and he seemed to start to say something, then glanced around at the street and held out a hand instead. "Thank you for doing this," he said.

Maggie took his hand. "You're welcome."

"I'll see you tomorrow afternoon," he said as he opened his door. "There's a set of spare keys to the house in a blue bowl in the hall."

Maggie nodded, then watched them back out of the driveway. Boudreaux had turned the corner by the time Maggie had retrieved her overnight bag and purse from the Jeep, and she turned and headed up to the front porch.

The breeze off the bay rattled through the Palmettos on either side of the front steps, and brought with it hints of brine and water grasses and mud. Maggie closed and

locked the front door behind her, and stared at the entry-
way.

She was at loose ends. She was in a foreign place, without anyone of her own nearby. It was too quiet, and too
empty, and too unfamiliar.

Her boots echoed up and down the hall as she made her
way to the stairs, then went up to the second floor. Yesterday, Boudreaux had shown her the guest room he'd had
Amelia make up for her. She found it again, and set her bag
on the white iron bed. She was grateful for the open windows, for both the fresh air and the reassurance that the
world outside was still there.

She looked around at the room, at the original wood
floors, the ship's lath walls left a chipped and faded tur-
quoise, the handmade quilt on the bed. There were no
books, there was no TV or phone.

She walked into the bathroom. Two bright white towels
hung over the side of a cast iron tub, and a small bowl of
soaps and lotions sat on the antique dresser that served as
a vanity. It was all very charming and understated, but she
felt too out of place to think about lying naked in the tub.
Instead, she turned around and went back out into the hall.

She walked opposite of the way she'd come, toward the
back stairs that led down to the kitchen. The double doors
of the room next to hers were open, and she couldn't help
stopping in the doorway. Boudreaux's room, she knew.

It was spotless and spare, as she would have expected
from such an immaculate man. The king-sized bed was of
antique mahogany, though understated in design, and covered with a gray-blue spread. The windows of this room
were open, too, and cream-colored, floor length sheers
moved gently against the wood floor.

There were no toiletries or dirty laundry to make the
room look lived in. The antique dresser held only a large

model of a shrimp boat. Through an open doorway beside the bed, Maggie saw a bathroom that was just as bare of superfluous decoration or detritus.

She was sorely tempted to open the nightstand drawers, to poke through the bathroom vanity, to gain the knowledge and intimacy that comes from going through another's things. She resisted that temptation by walking away.

Once downstairs in the kitchen, Maggie opened the big commercial fridge as if she might eat, but she wasn't hungry. The strange surroundings, Zoe's pain, and Wyatt's uncharacteristic unavailability, however deserved, made the idea of food unappealing.

She closed the door, then checked her phone again, in the way that people do when they hope they missed a call or accidentally turned off their ringer, but know they haven't done either. Nothing. She slipped it into the back pocket of her jeans, then opened the back door and stepped out onto the back porch.

Here, she felt more like she was on familiar ground. She'd spent quite a bit of time on this porch with Boudreaux, and she could almost hear echoes of conversations past, smell the mangos that had gone away until next summer.

Across the back yard, at the end of a brick-paved walkway, was a small cottage, lights on in every window but one. The front door was open, and as Maggie walked down the back steps and along the path, she could hear the faint sounds of television through the white, wrought-iron screen door.

It was loud once Maggie stood at the door, though she could see that the TV in the small living room was off. She knocked on the side of the door, but waited some time without an answer.

"Miss Evangeline?" she called. Again, there was no reply. Finally, she opened the door and went inside.

The main room was pleasant, in a slightly stereotypical Florida way. Furniture upholstered in tropical florals. Seascapes on the walls. This home was lived in though, with baskets of cross-stitch next to a recliner, well-read magazines on the bamboo coffee table, and a white sweater neatly folded on an ottoman.

There was an efficiency kitchen on one side of the room, and a closed door on the left wall. On the right, a small hallway, from which came the sounds of the TV.

"Miss Evangeline?" Maggie called again.

When she didn't get any answer, she went just to the hallway, and called a bit louder. "Miss Evangeline?"

"Who it is there?" the woman called from behind a closed door.

"It's Maggie Redmond," Maggie called back.

"Come in the door!" the woman yelled.

Maggie opened the door to find Miss Evangeline arranged beneath a heap of covers on a wicker twin bed, an old-fashioned pink rubber hot water bottle to one side of her, a box of candy to the other. The TV blared from the top of her dresser.

"I just came to see how you are," Maggie tried not to yell.

Miss Evangeline picked a remote up from the bed, pointed it at the TV. "Lemme slow the TV," she barked. "I can't hear nothin' you say, me."

She turned the volume down, and the Golden Girls stopped screaming at everybody.

"It's good to see you again, Miss Evangeline," Maggie said as she moved a little closer to the bed.

"I'm suppose be goin' home," Miss Evangeline huffed, "but Mr. Benny say I got to take care of you while he go."

Maggie tried not to smile, unsure if Miss Evangeline actually believed that, or even if Boudreaux had said it. She went to stand near the bed, glanced down at the night stand at a black and white photo in a silver frame.

In the picture, a woman in a bandana and a flowered housedress sat on a small wooden stool outdoors. It was undoubtedly Miss Evangeline, but she looked to be in her forties or so. On one side of her stood a young Creole girl, tall and straight, her arms folded across her chest. On the other stood a boy who was unmistakably Bennett Boudreaux.

"There go 'melia and Mr. Benny," Miss Evangeline said, following Maggie's gaze.

"May I look at it?"

"You lookin' at it already," Miss Evangeline said.

Maggie reached down and picked it up. Boudreaux appeared to be about Kyle's age, or maybe as old as twelve. He was wearing a white tee shirt and well-worn jeans and was barefooted. He was so tan that he was darker than the two light-skinned Creole women.

He was looking into the camera, and even from that distance, and in black and white, his eyes were arresting. But there was a look of sadness there that added to the weight Maggie already felt in her chest.

"Prettiest boy I ever saw," Miss Evangeline said.

Maggie nodded. He was pretty, pretty in the way that Kyle was, with those long, dark lashes and gentle features.

"Fifty-seven years I been raise him now," Miss Evangeline said. "Still he don't mind me, no."

Maggie smiled and set the picture back down.

"Come here eat of this chocolates," Miss Evangeline said, shaking the little gold box. "'Mr. Benny say he pay a million dollar to the Frenchmen for them chocolates, and I got to make it last. So I gon' eat ever one of these tonight, me."

She handed one delicate chocolate to Maggie. "You're not going to get sick are you?" Maggie asked.

"Sick for why?" the woman asked, the TV reflecting off of her thick lenses.

Maggie shook her head and put the chocolate in her mouth. It was luscious and silky and dark.

"Now you go the bed," Miss Evangeline said. At first Maggie thought she was supposed to sit, but Miss Evangeline was waving her off. "What day tomorrow is?"

"Thursday," Maggie said.

"Tomorrow ice cream day," the woman answered. "Mr. Benny take me out for the ice cream Thursdays."

Maggie wracked her brain for some memory of this in her myriad instructions, but came up empty. "Okay, we'll go get ice cream," she said. "I have some errands to run first."

"I go the errand," Miss Evangeline said, putting the last chocolate in her mouth.

"Yes," Maggie said. She was pretty sure it was assumed that she'd hang around the house all day with Miss Evangeline, but Boudreaux hadn't said not to take her anywhere, and she sure as heck wasn't leaving her alone.

"Is there anything you need before I go?" Maggie asked.

"I don't need nothin'," the old woman said. "I already had some water, and Mr. Benny fill up my douche bag," she said, holding up the hot water bottle.

Maggie stood there, glad she was too depressed and worried to burst out laughing or make a smart remark. "Well, good," she managed to say.

Miss Evangeline nodded, then set the empty box on her night stand.

"Good night, Miss Evangeline," Maggie said.

"'Night, girl," Miss Evangeline said, and turned the TV back up.

Maggie locked the front door before closing it, then headed back over to the big, empty house.

Zoe sat upright in her bed, propped up against her pillows. All of the lights in the house were off, except for a nightlight in the bathroom that cast a pale yellow glow into the hallway.

Zoe had been staring down the hallway for so long that her eyes felt scratchy and hot. She had been watching, expecting him to appear at the head of the hallway, so afraid of seeing him that sometimes she did, and her heart would pound for a moment or two. Every now and then, one of the cats would rattle their tags against their bowls in the kitchen, and a piece of Zoe would die.

Her muscles ached from hours of being ready to spring from her bed. She was slightly dizzy from breathing too shallowly for too long. She wanted her mother. She wanted her dad. She wanted to be someplace else, someplace where she didn't have to watch the hallway.

She was trying to get up the nerve to go close her bedroom door when the motion sensor light went off outside the window beside her bed, and everything that kept her alive stopped functioning at once.

Maggie took a long shower rather than a bath and pulled on a tank top and some plaid boxers. She placed her service weapon on the night stand out of habit, and slid into the white iron bed. The smooth, old sheets were cool and comforting, but she didn't feel comforted.

She checked her phone one more time, and contemplated calling Wyatt, but then set her alarm and waited for sleep to come. She was exhausted, yet wide awake.

After almost half an hour, she got back out of bed, grabbed her phone and her weapon, and went down to the kitchen for a glass of milk. When she'd finished it, she went on a wander, and found herself back at the door to Boudreaux's den.

The door was open, and Maggie stepped into the room. She set her phone and .45 on the ottoman, walked to the French doors and looked outside at the wind. Moonlight reflected off of the leaves of Boudreaux's many mango trees as they fluttered in the dark.

She turned back around and walked over to the couch where she'd sat last night. The denim blue sweater that Boudreaux had worn was tossed over the back. She reached out to feel its softness, then on impulse she picked it up and brought it up to her nose. It smelled just faintly of his elegant cologne.

After a moment's hesitation, Maggie slipped it over her head. The sleeves hung down several inches below her hands, and the bottom of the sweater covered her shorts. If she had thought he'd mind, she'd have taken it off, but somehow she didn't think he would. He was far too much the gentleman.

She curled up on the couch, and watched the trees with their dancing leaves until she finally fell asleep.

EIGHTEEN

Maggie awoke sore, tired, and momentarily lost.

Miss Evangeline was to have her breakfast on the table precisely at 8am, so Maggie got herself mentally resituated, dressed, made up the guest bed, and went down to the kitchen. If waking up alone in an unfamiliar place hadn't made her tense and cranky, struggling to understand and operate Boudreaux's coffee machine would have done the trick.

She finally managed to manufacture something at least physically drinkable, had a cup of coffee on the back porch, and then undertook to prepare Miss Evangeline's breakfast according to her daughter's instructions.

She finally got it on the table with four minutes to spare, poured herself another cup of coffee, and sat down with a copy of yesterday's paper that had been sitting on the counter.

A few minutes later, the back door opened, and an aluminum walker came through it, after a few preliminary bangs to the jamb on either side. It was followed eventually by Miss Evangeline, wearing a red bandana on her head and a blue flowered house dress on her frame.

Maggie stood and stepped hesitantly toward the woman, unsure if she needed help or would be insulted by it. She stopped halfway to her and let her proceed unaided.

"Good morning, Miss Evangeline," she said.

"Don't know it is," the old woman said. "Somebody put different tenny ball on my walkie-talkie, make it go too fast."

Maggie looked down at the tennis balls stuck onto the front pieces of the old lady's walker. They looked okay to her, and the only thing Miss Evangeline might outrun was a rock.

"Uh, well," Maggie said. "I don't know. I didn't do anything to them."

Miss Evangeline arrived at her chair at last, and Maggie couldn't help but take the lady's elbow as she sat. Miss Evangeline didn't seem to mind, or notice. Once the lady had navigated an actual seated position, Maggie walked back to her side of the table and sat down.

Maggie wasn't much of a social creature, and didn't seem to have the knack for small talk, especially with a near-stranger, so she had to cast about in her mind for something to say.

"Did you sleep well, Miss Evangeline?" she finally asked.

"Don't know," the woman said, peering suspiciously at her plate. "I miss the whole thing, me."

Maggie would have found that funny if she hadn't been so nervous about her ability to prepare one slice of maple bacon, dark not black, one slice of walnut-colored sourdough toast, and one over medium egg with no lace, no lace at all. She had an easier time cooking breakfast for ten than she did one tiny breakfast cooked to such specifications.

Miss Evangeline looked at her plate and then stared across the table. "Where your food at?"

"I don't eat breakfast," Maggie said. "Unless it's raw oysters."

The old lady stared at her a moment, and Maggie wondered if she'd grossed her out. But then Miss Evangeline dropped her eyes to her plate. The old woman stared at each component in turn, then finally picked up her fork and knife and began performing some kind of surgery on the egg. Maggie let out a breath and picked up the paper she'd been reading.

After a moment, she heard the dry-leaf voice from across the table.

"Somethin' wrong my egg," it said.

Maggie sighed quietly. She'd made and thrown away two other eggs before putting that one on the plate.

She lowered the newspaper. Miss Evangeline was picking at the egg with her fork.

"What, exactly?" Maggie asked.

Miss Evangeline looked up, her thick glasses almost opaque in the sunlight from the window.

"Got snots in it," she said. "The white all runny with snots."

Maggie blinked at her a few times. She'd labored over that stupid egg, making sure the white was "done, but not rubbery" and the yolk still slightly soft. She chewed at the corner of her lip and tried not to be snarky. It wasn't the old woman's fault that she was out of sorts.

"Would you like me to make you another one?"

Miss Evangeline looked back down at her plate. "I scrape the snots," she said.

"Okay," Maggie said. She took a healthy swallow of her coffee, then returned to the paper.

After a moment, Miss Evangeline spoke up again. "Bacon burned," she said.

Maggie lowered the paper. "No it isn't," she said.

The old lady stuck her face nearly on top of the bacon, then turned her Coke-bottle glasses back up at Maggie. "Too crisp. Gon' get underneath my teeths," she said.

Maggie sighed. "I followed Amelia's specifications exactly," she said. "Maybe I messed up the incantation."

Miss Evangeline stared blankly across the table, and Maggie lifted her paper back up. The story on Wyatt continued on the third page, and she flipped over to it.

"You thinkin' you big enough to sass me, then," she heard from the other side of the paper. She lowered it to find Miss Evangeline still staring at her.

"No, not at all," Maggie said. "I just know that I've never cooked a breakfast so carefully in my life."

"Careful, not careful, I don't know," Miss Evangeline said. "But you sass me again an' I come there and snatch you out that chair."

Maggie stared back at the old woman. For what felt like an eternity, neither of them blinked.

Finally, Maggie reached over and dragged the aluminum walker over to her side of the table, the tennis balls making a soft swish along the floor. Then she opened her paper back up.

"Come on, if you're coming," she said.

When Maggie and Miss Evangeline pulled into Zoe's driveway a short time later, Paulette was sitting on the front steps, drinking coffee and smoking.

Maggie told Miss Evangeline she'd just be a minute, and walked over to Paulette.

"Hey, Paulette. I just thought I'd drop in and check on Zoe."

"She's sleepin'," the woman answered. "She had a rough night."

"Is everything okay?"

The other woman drilled the cigarette into a small pail filled with cat litter. "Motion sensor went off last night," she said. "When I went out to look, it was just a possum goin' across the back yard."

Maggie let out a long breath and propped her hands on her hips as Paulette lit another cigarette.

"Girl was so scared, she couldn't even yell," Paulette said. "Woke me up bangin' on my wall."

Maggie felt a tremendous sense of guilt that she knew didn't necessarily belong to her, but she claimed it anyway. "Which light?"

"Her bedroom window," Paulette said.

Maggie started for the side yard. "I'll be right back."

Maggie walked around to the back yard. The kitchen, bathroom and Zoe's bedroom windows were all on the back wall of the duplex, Zoe's the last one she came to.

She stopped just to the side of the window and peered at the dirt beneath it, but she and her father had both been all over that spot the day before, and it was a mess of footprints, one on top of another.

She looked at Zoe's window, which was covered with mini-blinds, and said a silent prayer for the girl to get some decent rest. Her thoughts were interrupted by the vibration of her phone in her back pocket. She pulled it out and saw it was Wyatt, and didn't know if she was more nervous or relieved.

"Hey," she said when she answered.

"Hey. Where are you?"

"I'm at Zoe's. Her aunt says one of the motion sensors went off last night, so I'm looking around. Paulette says she saw a possum, but I didn't think it would be that sensitive."

"What motion sensors?"

"Daddy and Sky and I put some up yesterday," she said.

"Good," he said.

There was a long, unusual silence and Maggie was trying to come up with something to say when Wyatt finally spoke.

"Ignoring your calls was childish, but I needed some time to stop being mad," he said quietly.

"You don't owe me an apology, Wyatt," she said.

"I didn't give you one. I have every right to be mad, but I acted like an ass," he said. "I'm only sorry for that part."

"Well…" Maggie didn't know if she was supposed to apologize, accept his non-apology or just agree with him. "Are you still mad?"

"Yes, but less so," Wyatt said. "Boudreaux and I had a beer together yesterday and traded death threats. That helped me get some of it out."

"What?"

"Don't worry about it," he said.

"You don't trade death threats with Boudreaux!" Maggie said.

"You can," Wyatt said. "Although, mine wasn't nearly as smooth as his."

"Why did he threaten you?" Maggie said.

"I'm not certain, but I think it had something to do with telling him I'd kill him," Wyatt answered.

"For what?"

"For whatever presented itself," Wyatt said.

"Wyatt, he brought a knife to a gunfight and won," Maggie said stupidly. It had popped into her head.

"Yeah, I know," Wyatt said. "It's one of the few things I actually like about him."

"Crap," Maggie said.

"Let's move past that," Wyatt said. "What have you got going on today?"

"I'm taking Stoopid to the vet," Maggie answered. "Then I have to take Miss Evangeline to the Soda Fountain. Apparently Thursday is ice cream day. I might call the kids, see if they want to meet us after school."

"So I'm the only one who doesn't get ice cream," Wyatt said. "Because I threatened the mad dog killer whose nanny you're babysitting."

"Would you like ice cream?"

"I would."

"I'll call you when I get out of the vet. What are you doing?"

"I'm running down a couple of guys in Eastpoint who have taken a liking to joint flashings, then I'm working on a line-up for Zoe. I'll set it up for tomorrow," he answered.

"Okay," Maggie said.

"Okay," Wyatt said.

"Well, I'll see you," Maggie said.

"See you later," he said, then disconnected.

She was halfway across the back yard when her phone buzzed again.

"Real couples say 'I love you' before they hang up the phone," Wyatt said.

"Okay," she said.

"I love you," he said.

"I love you, too," she answered.

"We'll probably get the hang of it," he said, then hung up again.

NINETEEN

Miss Evangeline grimaced all the way down Maggie's dirt road, bouncing and jerking and holding onto the door handle, even though Maggie was doing 12mph. The old lady smiled, though, if the tectonic shifting of her features was any indication, once they pulled to a stop in front of the house.

"Look here this place, "Miss Evangeline said. "Pretty."

"Thank you," Maggie said. "I'll just be a second."

She reached into the back of the Jeep and grabbed an old beach towel, then got out of the car just as Coco came running down the stairs to meet her. Maggie waited for her, then rubbed her belly as she threw herself into the grass at Maggie's feet.

"That a Catahoula dog," Miss Evangeline said through her window.

"Yes," Maggie said. "Half Lab."

"Lou'siana dog," the old woman said.

"We got her on vacation in Grand Isle," Maggie said, as she watched Stoopid throw himself down the deck stairs like a bag of broken chopsticks.

Miss Evangeline cooed at Coco in what Maggie assumed was French, and Coco wagged over to the Jeep and sat, smiling up at the old lady. Maggie waited for Stoopid, the towel in her hands. He stopped within a few feet of her, flapped a few times, coughed out one of his crows, then commenced to peck at his chest. Maggie crept toward him, and he circled around her before returning his attention to his feathers.

"Somethin' wrong the boy chicken," Miss Evangeline piped up.

"I know," Maggie said quietly, slipping toward him again. "He's going to the vet."

She dropped the towel down onto Stoopid, who flapped and clucked and coughed as she folded his legs underneath him and wrapped him like a burrito. Once he was snugly wrapped, with nothing but his head sticking out, he calmed down.

Maggie told Coco to go upstairs, then got back into the Jeep and looked at Miss Evangeline. "Can you hold him?"

Miss Evangeline looked at her like she'd asked her to hold a bomb, then reached out and took the bundle, laid it on her lap. Maggie started the Jeep.

"Back where I come from, chicken broke, he don't go the doctor," she said. "He go the soup pot."

Maggie sighed, turned the Jeep around and headed back to the road.

⚓ ⚓ ⚓

They spent almost two hours in the waiting room, during which time Miss Evangeline diagnosed all of the animals and Stoopid had seven nervous breakdowns. In the end, they only spent ten minutes in the exam room, where Stoopid was found to have mites, mostly likely because he wouldn't leave the house long enough to take a dirt bath. It was also posited that he was a little high-strung, even for a rooster. Maggie was sent home with some mite spray and Stoopid was sent home wearing a miniature cone of shame. He seemed so demoralized by it that Maggie felt like she should have been given one, too.

She and Miss Evangeline made it to the Soda Fountain on Market Street just after school got out, and were shortly met by Sky and Kyle, who seemed somewhat charmed by Miss Evangeline. Maggie couldn't tell for sure, but she thought maybe it was mutual.

They took their ice cream cones outside so that Maggie could be within crowing distance of Stoopid. It was cool enough outdoors for him to be in the car a few minutes with the window cracked, but she'd let him out of the towel, and she imagined all manner of damage to her interior if he thought he'd been trapped and abandoned.

When Wyatt called to say he was on his way over the bridge, Maggie went inside to order his ice cream.

Market Street was fairly busy for a Thursday, owing mostly to out-of-towners who had come for the seafood festival, which started tomorrow. Passerby weaved around the small picnic table on the sidewalk where the kids and Miss Evangeline ate their ice cream, and Stoopid kept one eyeball glued to the window, ever alert for interlopers.

The two boys who approached them from Tamara's on the corner were in their early twenties. Their demeanor, all swagger and snicker, suggested they were at least of beer-drinking age. They were nearly abreast of both the picnic table and the Jeep when Stoopid hacked out something that could have been a greeting or an alarm.

"Crap, dude, check it out," one of the boys said, and they veered off the sidewalk and over to the passenger side of the Jeep.

The other boy, all over-styled hair and arrogant grin, laughed and tapped on the window. "Dude, free lunch," he said to his friend, as Stoopid tossed out a barrage of either news or insults.

"Hey!" Sky called over to them. "Leave him alone."

The kid at the window just grinned over at her, but his friend gave Sky an appreciative smile that wasn't appreciated. "Well, hey there," he said.

Sky got up as the other boy stuck his fingers through the cracked window, clucking at the rooster. "Back off," she said, walking between the two boys.

"Forget the chicken, man," the second boy said. "Check out the chick."

The first boy looked over at Sky and did a double take. "Hey, girl," he said, smiling.

Sky glared at him. "Get away from my mom's car, dude."

"If I do, will you come with me?" he asked, grinning.

Kyle stood up, and Miss Evangeline stood with him. "Stay put, little boy," she said. Then she yelled over at the two young men. "Go on, fool!"

The second of the two boys smiled over at Miss Evangeline, then back at Sky. "That your mom?" he asked.

"Get lost," Sky said, then turned around as the first boy tugged on her ponytail. "Don't touch me."

"Get away the girl, boy!" Miss Evangeline called. Kyle made to move forward, and Miss Evangeline put a hand on his shoulder.

"You wanna come hang out with us, sweetie?" the first boy asked Sky. "Party a little bit?"

"I got your party right here," the second boy said, resting a hand on the crotch of his jeans.

Sky looked down at his hand then back at his grin. "That looks like the kind of party a girl has to bring her own entertainment to," she said.

The boy's smile left his face as his friend laughed, and he tucked a finger under Sky's chin. "You think you're pretty funny, don't you?" he asked.

Kyle tossed his ice cream to the sidewalk as Sky slapped the boy's hand away, but Miss Evangeline grabbed him by the shirt and yanked him back, then reached into the pocket of her house dress.

Maggie walked out of the Soda Fountain just in time to register that two men were talking to her daughter, then watch one of them drop out of sight. She ran past her son and Miss Evangeline and around the Jeep to see the young man flat on his face on the asphalt, the two probes of a Taser attached to the space between his shoulder blades.

"What the hell is going on?" Maggie demanded.

The other man, a boy really, just gaped at her.

"Crap," Sky said, a look of wonder on her face.

Maggie was about to restate her question when Wyatt's cruiser stopped suddenly behind Maggie's Jeep.

Wyatt got out of his cruiser and stalked around the back end. Some kid was laid out at Sky and Maggie's feet with two probes stuck to him. Maggie was standing there staring, Sky was taking a picture with her phone, and E.T. was standing on the sidewalk with an ice cream cone in one hand and a yellow Taser in the other. He was about to ask what the hell happened when Stoopid popped up in the Jeep window with a little plastic cone around his neck, and Wyatt found himself with too many questions and not enough words.

"What happened, Sky?" Maggie asked.

"He put his hands on me," Sky said.

"Boy run his dirty mouth all over the chile," Miss Evangeline piped up. "I buzz him with my buzzer, me!"

The boy tried to roll over onto his back, and Wyatt yanked the probes from his shirt, then helped him over with a nudge of his foot.

"Call the police," the kid said weakly.

Wyatt bent over him and poked at the emblem on his polo. "We are the police, moron," he said. "Did you touch this girl?

"We didn't do nothin', man," the other boy said.

Maggie looked at Sky. "Sky?"

"He was bothering Stoopid and I told him to stop, then they started harassing me," her daughter answered.

"How old are you kid?" Wyatt asked the boy on the ground, who appeared to be thinking about sitting up. "Smells like you might have had a few beers."

"Twenty-one," he said weakly. "Old enough to have a beer."

"Too old to be hitting on a seventeen-year-old girl, though," Wyatt answered. "You wanna call us? Press charges against Methuselah's wife over there for zapping the crap out of you?"

The kid looked sullenly over toward Miss Evangeline, trying to look meaner than he was. Then he shook his head.

"Good," Wyatt said. He held out a hand, and the kid took it. Wyatt yanked him to his feet, but the kids knees buckled and he more or less dangled from Wyatt's grip. Wyatt looked at his friend. "Why don't you take your spider monkey home?"

They all watched as the kid led his friend away back the way they'd come.

Wyatt turned back to look at Maggie. "My week is a car-toon," he said.

"Wyatt, you should have seen it!" Kyle called excitedly.

"I think I've seen all I can take at this point," Wyatt answered. He looked at Maggie, standing there with her hands full of ice cream. "Is that my Rocky Road?"

"Yeah," she said, and handed it to him. Her own pine-apple sherbet was half melted, and she walked over to the sidewalk and tossed it into the trash. "Let's go, Kyle," she said. "Come on, Clint Eastwood."

Kyle hovered near Miss Evangeline until she'd managed to navigate herself and her walker off of the sidewalk.

"Boy, go get my slinkies for me" she said, pointing at her probes still lying on the ground.

Maggie looked at Sky. "Go home," she said, sighing.

"I didn't do anything," Sky said.

"I know. Just go home. I'll be there as soon as I can hand her off to her keepers."

She opened the passenger door of the Jeep, dropped the towel back onto Stoopid, wrapped him up, and handed him to Kyle. "Here."

"Is he in custody for something?" Wyatt asked.

"Mites," Maggie said shortly.

"Sure," Wyatt said.

Kyle handed Miss Evangeline her probes, then took Stoopid in his arms and followed Sky to her truck. Maggie looked up at Wyatt, who was licking his ice cream like he was at a parade.

"Bye," she said tiredly.

"Bye," he answered.

She walked around to her side of the Jeep and got in. "Come on, Miss Evangeline," she called.

Miss Evangeline tucked her Taser back into her pocket and headed for the Jeep at the speed of plant. "Boy a fool.

Touch that chile and don't even know who she is," she muttered. "Bones don't float, no."

Wyatt chewed a piece of walnut thoughtfully as he watched her fold her walker and get in, then he shut the door and walked to his cruiser. He pulled up far enough to let them out, then watched in his rear view as Maggie headed toward the Historic District.

TWENTY

M aggie waited on Boudreaux's back porch while he took his overnight bag upstairs and changed his clothes, then carried Amelia's bag out to the cottage.

Maggie watched him as he retraced his steps along the path from the cottage to the back porch. He had changed from his black suit into gray trousers and a white linen button-down shirt. Even when casually dressed for home, he was more elegant than Maggie had been at her own wedding.

He came up the back steps and smiled at Maggie. "Apparently, you've made an impression on Miss Evangeline. Again," he said.

"Oh, I'm sure I have," she said, watching him walk over to the small bamboo bar near the kitchen door.

"You ladies didn't have a set-to, did you?" he asked.

"Every conversation with her is a set-to," she said.

Boudreaux nodded his agreement. "And yet, she likes you," he said.

"I like her, too."

"Would you like a cocktail?" he asked her.

"I think I would," Maggie answered.

"I can make you a mojito if you like," he said. "I'm just having a Cape Cod."

"What is that?"

"Vodka and cranberry juice."

"That sounds fine," Maggie said. "Thank you."

He took some small cans of cranberry juice out of the mini-fridge and began making the drinks. Maggie rested her head against the back of the white Adirondack chair she was sitting in, closed her eyes a moment, and enjoyed the evening breeze, which was just shy of chilly.

"So how did it go?" Boudreaux asked as he mixed their drinks.

"Well, I can't fry an egg or cook a slice of bacon properly," Maggie said, her eyes still closed.

"Who can, really?" Boudreaux said.

"But I *should* cook my rooster," she added, opening her eyes. Boudreaux started across the porch with their drinks. "It went pretty well, until she Tasered somebody on Market Street."

Boudreaux handed her her cocktail, took a swallow of his, and pinched at the bridge of his nose before he hit her with those eyes. "What was she doing on Market Street?"

"Thursday is ice cream day." Maggie took a swallow of her drink.

"No, Saturday was ice cream day. Twenty years ago," Boudreaux said. "She's too senile, ornery, and armed to go anywhere now."

Boudreaux sat down in the chair next to her.

"You didn't tell me she was a con artist," Maggie said.

"She's so many things," he said. "Who did she Taser?"

"Some jerk that needed it," Maggie said. "It was over-kill, but not completely uncalled for."

"Are they pressing charges?"

"No."

Boudreaux looked at her a moment, frowning. "Did someone do something to you?"

"No, it was just some guys from out of town, harassing Sky," she said. "She could have dealt with it." Boudreaux took another sip of his drink. Maggie looked over at him. "How was Louisiana?"

"It was fine," he said. "Funeral notwithstanding."

Maggie took a drink as she watched him. "Did you see your wife?"

"I must look like hell for you to ask me that," he said.

"You look fine," she replied.

"No. We have spoken on the phone once or twice, when absolutely necessary," Boudreaux said. "But I haven't seen her since July."

"Did she leave you?"

"No. No, she's not going to leave her credit cards and her big house and her allowance," he said.

Maggie stared at him for a moment. "Why did you marry her at all? You said you've never been in love."

Boudreaux took a sip of his drink. "She was a young widow from an old, politically-connected society family that had run out of money," he said. "I was starting to make money, but I was an overeducated Cajun boy from the bayou. We served each other's needs at the time."

"You know it's incongruous that you won't divorce her because you're Catholic, right?"

"I know that, yes," he said. "But, despite the fact that I no longer need her family's connections, I don't see how getting divorced would benefit me."

Maggie looked at him a moment, thought about her words. "Maybe you wouldn't be so sad," she said finally.

"Do you think my marriage makes me sad, Maggie?" he asked quietly.

"I think being alone makes you sad," she said.

He looked at her over his glass as he took a long sip of his drink. The wind blew a small handful of hair across his forehead, and he ran a hand through it before he spoke.

"Perhaps that's one of the things that draws us to each other," he said. "We see a sadness in each other that we want to repair."

"I have a wonderful life," Maggie said. "I have a great family, and Wyatt."

"And yet…" Boudreaux said.

"And yet, what?"

"You tell me," he said.

"Maybe I'm a little sad sometimes," she said. He waited, and she took a healthy swallow of her drink, stared at her fingerprints in the condensation on the glass. "I get this weariness, deep in my bones, when I think about another fifteen or twenty years in this line of work," she said quietly. "That's so many dead and broken people, so many grieving families."

She set the glass down on the arm of the chair and glanced over at Boudreaux. He sat quietly, drink in his lap, his chin on his free hand.

"So many images I'll wish I could bleach from my memory," she added.

Boudreaux stared back at her a moment before speaking. "I suspect you'll do it, though. I think you need to help people."

Maggie shook her head slightly. "*Helping people* is keeping horrible things from happening. That's not what I do. I come in after the horrible things. The best I can hope for is to put someone in jail."

"Aren't you underestimating the value of justice?" he asked.

"No, I just know that justice doesn't put people back the way they were," she answered.

"Perhaps not," Boudreaux answered. "But doing nothing isn't an answer."

Maggie wanted to say something sharp, but caught herself. She wasn't angry with Boudreaux, she was angry with the world.

"It takes something out of me," she said instead. "This case I'm on now is taking something out of me." She looked over at him. "A young girl I used to know. Raped."

"How old?" Boudreaux asked.

"Fourteen," she said.

"A year younger than you were," he said quietly.

"Yes. And even if we catch this guy, even if he's indicted for first degree sexual battery of a minor, he'll probably cop a plea, or have some doctor there to tell the jury how disadvantaged or damaged he is. At best, he'll get sentenced to thirty years and do ten, still be a young man when he gets out."

"Well, if you find out who he is, you could always just let me know instead."

Maggie turned back to look at him, her brows knitting together. Boudreaux gave her a slight smile.

"I'm a cop," Maggie said, only a little surprised. "I'm not going to have you kill a rape suspect."

Boudreaux calmly took a swallow of his drink. "I expected as much," he said mildly. "But it would have been impolite of me not to offer."

Zoe sat on the edge of the upholstered chair in the living room, holding her cell phone in one hand and petting the gray cat in her lap with the other. She sat ramrod straight, her ears listening for every sound in her immediate environment, as they had been doing all day.

It had been Aunt Paulette's first day back at work, and Zoe hadn't been able to do anything but watch and listen, even in the light of day. She turned on the TV for company, then turned it off because she was afraid it would mask other, stealthy noises. She desperately wanted a shower, but the idea of being naked while alone in the house was out of the question. She would wait. If she had to wait until tomorrow, she would wait.

Her aunt had called to check on her around five, had said she'd be home shortly, but it was now almost eight and she wasn't there. This would not have surprised Zoe last week, and it didn't surprise her tonight as much as she wished it would. She knew Paulette had stopped at one of her friends' houses, to drink beer and maybe smoke a little. Her hope now was that she'd be home before dark, but dark was well on its way, and Zoe was starting to wonder how she was going to stand being so watchful for so long.

There were no groceries to speak of in the house, so Zoe had called and ordered a pizza. After eating pizza two or three times a week for the last several months, Zoe was sick to death of it, but she was hungry. She'd used the debit card her aunt left at home for just in case, and ordered sausage even though she didn't like it much. It was silly, she knew, but she thought maybe if she ordered Paulette's favorite, the woman would miraculously appear, saying she was sorry to be so late, but the lines at Piggly-Wiggly had been long.

Zoe heard the gravel crunching out front, dumped the cat from her lap, and ran to the front window. She had hoped it would be her aunt getting dropped off, but it was just the pizza guy, a young guy around twenty-five or so, with bleached blond hair. He'd delivered to her many times before. She opened the door as he jogged up the sidewalk.

"Hey, how are you?" he asked cheerfully. "Here you go, fresh and hot."

Zoe tried for a real smile, but she knew it was only a tight, polite one. "Thank you," she said.

She waited as he opened the insulated bag, and she didn't know if it was the smell or what, but she was suddenly slightly nauseous and sorry she'd ordered the thing.

"Extra sausage, extra cheese are in the house," he said pleasantly as he pulled the pizza from the bag.

Zoe stared at the box. Every hair on her body was electrified. She was cold and hot, suddenly and simultaneously. The phrase "in the house" seemed to burn into her ears and down her throat.

"It smells good," she said, and her voice sounded very small, and very far away.

She kept her eyes on the pizza, saw his hand as he put her credit card receipt and a ball point pen on top.

"Here you go. Just sign the top one and the bottom one's yours," he said. Zoe felt bile rising, and was suddenly afraid that she was going to vomit.

"Thank you," she said again, from somewhere else.

She reached out and took the pen, though she didn't want to touch it, didn't want to touch it, didn't want to touch it. She watched her hand shake as she remembered to add a tip, then signed her aunt's name. The pen trembled as she held it out. He didn't take it right away, and she was forced to look up. He was staring at her, his smile much smaller, barely there.

"Sorry," she said, smiling weakly. "I've been sick for a few days."

He put most of his smile back in place. "I'm sorry to hear that," he said politely. "Glad you've got your appetite."

He held out the pizza, and she took it from him. She was so aware of the horribly small distance between them that she could physically feel it adjust when he backed down one stair.

"You have a nice night now," he said.

"You, too," she said, then made herself close the door gently and lock it, like a regular person would do in the regular world. Then she threw the pizza onto the floor and ran to the front window. Her hot, panicked breaths bounced off the curtains and back into her face as she tilted her ear at the window and waited for the sound of his car. She wasn't sure her heart was still beating until he finally pulled away, and then her heart began pounding so hard that she thought she might faint. She peeked out the window, afraid it was some kind of trick, but he was gone.

She ran to the back door. From just a few feet away she could see that it was still locked, but she jerked at the knob anyway, checked that the sliding lock above the door knob was tight. There were sounds coming out of her that she didn't recognize, sounds that had no meaning to her, but she couldn't stop herself from making them.

She tripped over one of the cats as she turned to run back to the living room, and found herself sprawled on the tile floor near the dining room table. She didn't feel her bottom teeth as they cut her lower lip; all she knew was that she must not be on the floor.

She half climbed, half crawled into the living room, managing to get to her feet as she reached the chair she'd been sitting in. She snatched up her phone. It took her trembling fingers three tries before she got her password right, and she nearly screamed before they did. She could hear her voice in her ears, but for some reason she couldn't understand what she was saying.

She found her recent calls screen, and had to tap the number several times before she got it to go.

TWENTY-ONE

M aggie was on 12th Street, just passing Weems Memorial on her way home, when her cell rang from the passenger seat. She glanced over long enough to see that it was Zoe, answer it, and hit the speaker button. "Hey, Zoe," she said, as she crossed Avenue I.

At first, all she could make out was a low, breathy, grunting sound, and her heart leaped up into her throat.

"Zoe? Zoe!" she yelled.

Zoe made some noises that sounded like "unh, unh, unh" and Maggie barely managed to look both ways before she floored it through the next stop sign.

"Zoe!" she yelled again. "Talk to me!"

"It—it—it's the pizza man, it's the pizza man," the girl finally blurted out.

Maggie reached over and turned on her dash light, flipped the siren. "Is he there?" she yelled.

"He was here! He was here!"

"Is your aunt there?"

"N—no," the girl answered, and Maggie could hear her gagging or trying to catch her breath.

"Three blocks, Zoe!" Maggie called, trying to sound calmer. "I'm right there! Three blocks!"

She reached over and grabbed her handset, keyed her radio, and forced her voice to be steady and slow. "Franklin 100 to Franklin," she said.

"Go ahead, Franklin 100," the dispatcher responded.

"10-12 with subject by phone, two-zero-two one-two street, subject was at the residence, may still be in the area. Requesting back-up."

"10-4, Franklin 100," the dispatcher responded. "Franklin 103, Franklin."

Maggie heard Carl Pitasniak respond. "Franklin 103, 10-18, 10-51."

Maggie could hear Zoe gasping for breath over her phone's speaker, and she forced herself to speak calmly. "Zoe, I'm almost there."

"Franklin 1 to Franklin," Wyatt's calm voice said over the radio. "10-51, 10-18 to Franklin 100's location."

Maggie felt a certain comfort in that, as she whipped into the housing development, mindful of her speed in a neighborhood where kids still played outside. She threw the Jeep into park, grabbed her Glock 23 from her purse on the seat. She snatched up her phone, and was out her door while the gravel was still settling.

"Zoe, I'm here! Open the door, baby," she said into the phone.

She heard a siren not far off as she reached Zoe's steps, then the door was yanked open. Zoe was wild-eyed, clutching her phone to her chest. She was about to say something to Maggie, then just started taking in long, sucking breaths. Maggie stepped inside and wrapped her arms around the girl.

"It's okay. It's okay," Maggie said. She held the girl away from her. "Was he inside? When was he here?"

"No, he just delivered the pizza," Zoe said. "Like five, ten minutes ago."

Maggie stuck her weapon in the back of her jeans and put her hands on Zoe's face."What happened?"

It took Zoe a moment to answer. Maggie watched her try to slow her breathing enough to speak. "I ordered a pizza. From the place we always get pizza. It was him, the guy that delivers the pizzas."

"Which pizza place?" Maggie answered. Zoe looked past Maggie at the floor and Maggie turned around. There was a pizza box on the floor, half crushed. Pizza One. She looked back at Zoe. "What happened?"

"I left him a tip," Zoe said. "I remembered to leave him a tip."

"What? Did he know you recognized him, Zoe?"

"I don't know. I'm not sure," Zoe answered, and Maggie could feel her ratcheting up again. Behind her, she heard a siren approaching, and then the crunching of tires on gravel.

"Zoe, how'd you recognize him?"

"His voice," Zoe answered, squeezing her eyes shut. "He said something about the house and I recognized his voice. Maybe an accent. I don't know, but I know it was him."

"Zoe, look at me," Maggie said calmly. "I'm here. You're okay."

Zoe nodded, then looked over Maggie's shoulder. Maggie turned to see Wyatt stalking up the sidewalk. She stepped toward the door as Wyatt came up the steps.

"It was a delivery guy from Pizza One," Maggie said. "He brought a pizza maybe ten minutes ago."

"She make him for sure?" Wyatt asked.

"She thinks so." Maggie turned to Zoe. "What does he look like?"

Zoe stared past Wyatt at the open doorway. "He was maybe twenty, twenty-two? He has really blond hair, like fake blond. Brown eyes." She held her hand up above her head. "About this tall. Not skinny, but not built."

"Fits," Wyatt said quietly.

Maggie turned and looked past Wyatt as a cruiser pulled in behind Wyatt, followed more slowly by a red Skylark. Carl Pitasniak got out of the cruiser and headed for the house. Wyatt went to talk to him, met him halfway down the sidewalk.

Paulette Boatwright got out of the passenger side of the Skylark hesitantly, then hurriedly shut the door as the car backed out of the driveway.

Maggie stalked out the door and past Wyatt and Carl.

"Where were you?' Maggie demanded.

Paulette looked frightened. "I was at work. What happened?"

"You work from eight to four!" Maggie snapped. "Where were you?"

"I just stopped—"

"You're high, dammit!! Maggie said.

"Maggie," Wyatt said behind her.

Maggie ignored him. "You selfish—"

"Maggie!" Wyatt said more loudly. "Not now."

Maggie poked a finger in Paulette's direction. "If I could charge you, I would," she said. In truth, she felt maybe she would have shot her if she could.

"What happened?" Paulette called.

Maggie's boots clumped along the sidewalk as she walked back to the house. Zoe backed up as Maggie went back inside.

"Do you want to come with me?" she asked, sounding angrier than she meant to.

Zoe looked out the front door, where Paulette was talking to Wyatt as she tried to light a cigarette. The woman was weaving a bit.

"Okay," Zoe said.

"Go pack a bag," Maggie said. "Bring your school stuff."

"How much do you want me to pack?"

Maggie shook her head. "Just pack for a few days. You can wash clothes if you need to."

She watched Zoe head for the hallway, then she stepped back outside. Wyatt walked away from Paulette and met Maggie halfway. "Forget about the aunt," he said.

"Forgotten."

"We're gonna head over to Pizza One," Wyatt said. "Dwight's gonna meet us over there."

"Zoe's coming with me," Maggie said.

"You need the aunt's permission. She's not sixteen. Unless you want to call DCS, and that's a whole different can of hell."

"I'm not calling DCS," Maggie said, already walking away. She stopped in front of Paulette. "Do I have your permission to take Zoe with me?"

Paulette blew out some smoke. She looked more scared than someone that high usually did. "Like protective custody?"

"I'm just taking her with me," Maggie said shortly. "I have your permission, right?"

Paulette glanced over Maggie's shoulder at Wyatt, then back at her. "You think I'm a bad person," she said.

"I'm not thinking about you," Maggie answered. "Do I have your permission to take Zoe with me for a few days or not?"

Paulette focused a moment. "Go on, then," she said.

Maggie turned back around. "When are you going?" she said to Wyatt.

"As soon as you pull out," Wyatt said.

"I'm fine, Wyatt," she said.

"I know that," he said.

He followed her back to the house. Maggie kicked the pizza box aside and walked down the hallway to Zoe's room, then stopped in the doorway. Zoe was standing in the corner, between her closet and the wall, a couple of hangers with tops on them clutched to her chest.

"Zoe?" Maggie asked.

"I can't move," the girl said quietly.

Maggie stepped into the room. Zoe's bag sat open on the bed, a hodgepodge of items thrown into it.

"It's okay, baby," Maggie said gently. She felt Wyatt come in behind her, glanced back at him, then looked at Zoe. "This is Sheriff Hamilton. Wyatt. He's my friend."

Zoe looked at Wyatt, then back to Maggie. "He was right there," Zoe said.

"I know. But he's gone."

"I can't move," Zoe repeated.

Wyatt stepped past Maggie, stopped a foot away from Zoe, and held out his hand. "Zoe? Can I help you?" he asked gently.

After a moment, Zoe took his hand. Wyatt made as though to step back and walk her to the car, but she went to him and dropped her face on his chest, still clutching her hangers. Wyatt bent and picked her up, and turned to leave.

"Get the rest of her stuff," he said quietly as he walked past Maggie.

Maggie grabbed a toothbrush and tube of toothpaste from the bedspread, tossed them into the overnight bag, then rifled for a moment to see if Zoe had the basics. She'd forgotten to pack any underwear, so Maggie found some in her dresser and tossed them in. She was about to zip up the bag when she saw the beaten-up brown teddy bear near the pillow. She tossed him in, too, then grabbed Zoe's bag and headed out.

When she got back to the living room, Paulette was sitting on the loveseat, her cigarettes in her hand. She looked up at Maggie, and her expression was an odd blend of shame, regret, and defiance.

Maggie was going to walk right past her, but she stopped. The woman didn't look away, and Maggie had to give her credit for that at least.

"You need to get it together," Maggie said. "Neither one of you has anybody else, and having nobody sucks." She closed the front door behind her as she went out.

Wyatt was talking to Carl next to Maggie's Jeep. Zoe sat in the passenger seat. At the road, Dwight was shooing a few looky-loos back to their homes.

"Zoe says she doesn't remember what the guy drives." Wyatt said when she approached. "If he's not at the pizza place, we'll get that info from them."

"Who else is going?" Maggie asked.

"Carl and Dwight. Jackson from PD is meeting us over there," Wyatt said. He looked over at Carl. "Let's go. Dwight!"

"Call me," Maggie said, and Wyatt held a hand up to acknowledge he'd heard her. She got in and started the Jeep, and Wyatt waited for her to back out, then did the same.

She looked in the rearview once she got to 12th Street. Wyatt and the deputies were all behind her. They stayed behind her until they got to Main, then Maggie turned right and everyone else turned left.

There was quite a lot of traffic on the road, everyone piling into town for the Seafood Festival, or already there and looking for dinner. Maggie checked her rearview a few times, but didn't see anyone who appeared to be following them.

A few minutes later, she waited for traffic to pass, checked the rear view again just before turning, then pulled onto her parents' driveway.

"Is this your house?" Zoe asked.

"No, this is where I grew up," Maggie said. "My parents' house. I live out in the middle of nowhere, and I may need to go back out later. Is this okay?"

Maggie glanced back at the road in her rearview. No one turned into her parents' driveway, and no one seemed to slow as they passed.

"If you go out, are you coming back?"

"Yes," Maggie said. "I'll stay here with you."

"Where are Sky and…your son?"

"Kyle. They're at home." Maggie pulled to a stop in front of the house and turned off the engine. "But they're supposed to be spending the night here. We're all going to the Seafood Festival tomorrow. Are you okay with them being here, too?"

"Yeah. I mean, I guess," Zoe said. "Having people around kind of sounds good right now."

Maggie looked at her for a moment. "You and I can just stay here tomorrow, if you don't feel like being out in a crowd," she said.

Zoe thought about that for a moment. "No, it's okay," she said.

"Okay," Maggie said.

They got out of the Jeep. Maggie grabbed Zoe's bag, and they headed for the front porch.

A few hundred feet short of the Redmonds' driveway, an older blue Maxima with a Pizza One sign on the back seat sat idling in a gas station parking lot.

TWENTY-TWO

M aggie and her father were sitting out on her parents' back deck, drinking sweet tea and listening to the bug zapper zap bugs. Behind them, they could hear Maggie's mother Georgia talking to Kyle as she worked a puzzle with him at the kitchen table. Out in the back yard, Sky and Zoe sat close together under a Sabal palm, deep in conversation.

Maggie watched them from where she sat on the bottom step, until her phone buzzed beside her. It was Wyatt.

"Did you get him?" she asked.

"His name is Michael Finch, and no. He never came back to the pizza place," Wyatt said. "In fact, he never delivered the other three pizzas he was carrying."

"He knew," she said.

"Yeah. We had to get the owner down here to access the employee records, but we got his address. Over here on Sixth Street. He's not here, either. However, we put a BOLO out on his blue Maxima, and Apalach PD just called it in. It's at a trailer over on 25th Avenue."

"Are you on your way already?" Maggie asked, standing up.

"Yep."

"I'm coming," Maggie said, already headed down the steps.

Wyatt gave her the address, which was only about a mile and a half away. "About a hundred yards south on the left, there's an empty trailer. Meet us in the driveway."

⚓ ⚓ ⚓

It only took Maggie a few minutes to make it to the spot where Wyatt, Dwight, and two Apalach PD officers were waiting. It was a long gravel driveway leading to a dilapidated brown trailer with a few old tires and an oil drum in the yard. In between it and the trailer they were headed to was an empty wooded lot.

Wyatt and the others were standing by Wyatt's cruiser. Maggie got out, carrying her body armor with her, and joined them.

"We've got two other cars in the yard over there," Wyatt said, "in addition to the Maxima. They might run, they might not. They might have drivers, they might not. Safer to expect they run and have both drivers and passengers."

Sgt. Bret Woods from PD looked at Maggie. "Like I told Wyatt, what we have here is Dwayne Charles's place. He's a small-time pot dealer, typical burn-out. Never been violent, as far as I know."

Maggie nodded as she pulled the Velcro on her armor tight.

"Let's go ahead and assume everyone is in a pissed-off violent mood, okay?" Wyatt said quietly.

Wyatt had his black vest on over his polo. Dwight wore his over his uniform shirt, as did the two PD officers.

"If he's gonna run, he'll run out the back," Wyatt said. "Bret, you and I will take the back, Maggie, Dwight, and Bill will go in the front." Everyone nodded. Wyatt crooked a finger at Maggie. "You, come with me for a minute."

Maggie followed him back over to the far side of her Jeep. Wyatt turned around and frowned at her.

"I'm thinking I'll be okay with this guy resisting arrest," Wyatt said, as he tugged on the Velcro straps of her vest. "I'm also thinking I'm okay with this job change. I'm not too enthusiastic about letting you go through doors anymore, much less ordering you to do it."

Maggie swallowed, had a sudden flash of him lying on his kitchen floor, covered in blood and paler than the tile. "Well, I'll be kind of happy when you aren't doing it, either."

"Maybe we should both get out," he said.

"I'll put my app in at Piggly-Wiggly," she said.

"Lie about your people skills," he said.

He looked at her and sighed. Maggie tried to smile. Cops on TV barreled through doors into unknown situations like they were crashing a toddler's birthday party. The reality was that it was scary, every single time, like jumping blindfolded into a tank that probably held sharks.

"Okay, well," Wyatt said.

"Yep," Maggie said, and followed him back to the guys. Thirty seconds later, they were headed through the wooded lot next door.

⚓ ⚓ ⚓

Maggie and Dwight stood on either side of the trailer's battered door, weapons at the ready. There was only room for two on the trailer's tiny front deck. Bill waited at the bottom of the two steps. They could hear Nirvana playing, even though the windows were shut.

Maggie looked at Dwight's profile as he stared at the door. She was almost ten years older than Dwight, but she'd known him since he was a teenager. He had a sweet wife who did cross-stitch, and three kids under the age of seven. He was the first male in his family to do something other than shrimping.

Maggie swallowed, closed her eyes for one moment, and then used her weapon to knock on the door. They could hear shuffling inside, then someone turned the music down.

"Who is it?" a male voice called, and Maggie could tell he was at least a few feet from the door.

"Franklin County Sheriff's Office. Open the door," Maggie called.

There was more shuffling, and the thumping of feet trying unsuccessfully to be quiet on the thin floors of the trailer. Dwight looked at Maggie and she nodded. He kicked in the door, and they went through it. A few seconds later, Maggie heard the back door slam open.

Wyatt was standing on the concrete blocks that served as steps when the back door swung open and a kid with long, dyed black hair flew through it. Wyatt stuck out his arm and clotheslined the kid, who went down hard on the kitchen floor.

"Stop," Wyatt said quietly, and went through the door as Bret ran up the blocks. The kitchen was open to the living room, and Wyatt saw Maggie pointing her weapon at two guys standing against an entertainment center. One had orange hair, the other none at all.

The pot cloud was enough to get them all high, and Wyatt coughed as he stepped over the black-haired kid, who looked like he was trying to back into the cupboard under the sink. Wyatt pointed at him. "Up."

The kid stood up, hands in the air, and Bret patted him down.

"In the living room," Wyatt told him.

The kid held up his hands, which were shaking violently, and walked in front of Wyatt. Bret followed them into the living room, and they arrived as Dwight came into the room from a hallway.

"That's it," Dwight said.

"What's going on, man?" a skinny kid guy with orange hair and a brown goatee asked.

"Michael Finch," Maggie said.

"He ain't here," the kid said.

"His car is," Maggie said.

Wyatt shoved the black-haired kid toward his friends. "Which one of you citizens is Dwayne?"

The guys just stood there. "The kid with the goatee," Bret said. The kid with the goatee looked unhappy.

"Where's Finch?" Wyatt asked him, as Dwight and Bret began patting the men down.

"I don't know, man," Dwayne said. "What the hell."

"He left, dude," the bald guy said. He appeared to be a few years older than the others.

"When?" Maggie asked.

"Like an hour ago," Dwayne answered.

"Without his car?" Wyatt asked.

"He sold it to me for four hundred bucks," Dwayne said. "He said he needed the cash to get out of town."

"How's he getting out of town without his car, Dwayne?" Maggie asked.

"His bike, man," the kid answered. "I was holding his bike for him 'cause he doesn't have a driveway or nothin' at his place."

"What kind of bike?"

"I don't know man. Some not-Harley kind of bike," the kid said.

"It was some kind of Kawasaki," the bald guy said. "Crotch rocket. Black."

"Where'd he say he's going?" Wyatt asked, as he poured what was left of a can of Diet Coke into an ashtray that was about to burst into flames.

"He didn't say, dude," the black-haired kid said.

"What'd he do, man?" the bald guy asked.

"He was rude," Wyatt said. "Do *you* know where he went?"

"No, man," the guy answered.

"You wouldn't lie to me?" Wyatt asked. "Because I couldn't care less at the moment how much weed you're holding, but if you hand me crap you'll all be getting cavity searched within the hour."

"I swear, man," the bald guy said. "I barely know the dude."

Wyatt sighed and looked at Bret. "Can you get IDs and license plates?" he asked.

"Yeah," Bret answered.

"Maggie, Dwight," Wyatt said, and they followed him out the front door and into the yard.

"You buy what they're saying?" Maggie asked.

"Yeah, but I don't know that I buy what he told them," Wyatt said.

"Me, neither," she said.

"More than likely, he is hauling ass. I just don't like that we don't know that." Wyatt looked at Dwight. "Dwight, go on back to the office, see if we can get a license plate for this guy's motorcycle. Then go ahead and file a preliminary and go home."

"Gotcha, boss," Dwight said. "This was fun and all," he added as he headed back to the woods.

Wyatt looked at Maggie, who was chewing on the corner of her lip. "What's on your mind?" he asked her.

Maggie shook her head. "I don't like that he delivered the pizza," she said.

"Talk to me about that."

"Would you have delivered a pizza?"

"I don't think they get to pick their deliveries, but no. And yeah, it's troubling."

"I'm wondering if this guy isn't a typical rapist," Maggie said.

"Because he came back?"

"I think maybe the possum was convenient, but it wasn't alone," she said. "And I think he fully expected to have to deliver another pizza over there. He wanted to."

"You think his thing is to mess with her head?"

"I keep going back to the leaves," Maggie said.

"Okay," Wyatt said.

"Dr. Callahan said it could have been some kind of repair, like he was trying to undo taking her virginity, like he was putting it back," Maggie said. "But what if he was putting it back so he could take it again?"

Wyatt looked at her and sighed. "We think a lot of sick crap," he said.

"We know a lot of sick crap," she said.

Wyatt put his hands on his hips and huffed out a breath. "I'm gonna wait on the guys and see about keeping this place under eyeballs for a bit," he said. "Finch could come back, or one of these Stanford applicants could try to go see him."

"Okay," Maggie said. "I need to get back to Zoe. I feel bad. I know she feels out of place."

"She's safe," Wyatt said.

"Yeah," she said. And Zoe was; Daddy could work that .38 revolver of his just as swiftly as he did a shucking knife. "Okay, I'll see you later."

"See you later."

Maggie crossed the yard, heard Wyatt going back up the trailer stairs, as she stepped into the wooded lot.

The wind had picked up some, and the tall, skinny pines were all whispering the secrets that trees tell. 25th Avenue was quiet, and Maggie listened to her boots crunching through the pine needles, pine cones, and dead leaves as she made her way through the woods.

She looked up through the trees, saw the moon glowing above her. She thought about Zoe lying in the dirt looking up through the treetops, looking at the same moon. Thought of herself lying in different woods, at a different time, staring up at the cloudless, blue November sky and wishing she was looking at it from somewhere else.

She brushed at her arms, quickened her step, and hurried through to the other side.

TWENTY-THREE

When Maggie got back to her parents' house, most of the house was dark except for the kitchen, where Gray sat at the table playing cards with Zoe. Her dad was up by five every morning and in bed by ten. Maggie knew he'd stayed up for Zoe, and she loved him for it.

They both looked up as she walked into the kitchen.

"What happened?" Zoe asked. "Is he in jail?"

Maggie put her purse down on the counter and sighed. "No, I'm sorry. He isn't," she said. "He might have left town."

Zoe just sat there, eyes wide, and Gray gently laid a hand on her shoulder. "Wyatt and Maggie will find him," he said.

Maggie knew that very well might be a lie, and she wished he hadn't said it, but she knew he felt he had to say something.

"Everybody's looking for him, Zoe," she said quietly.

Zoe nodded, and Gray patted her shoulder and pushed back his chair. "I'll let the two of you talk," he said as he stood. "Try to get some sleep tonight, Zoe. You're okay here."

Zoe nodded. "Thank you, sir," she said, her voice barely above a whisper.

Maggie watched Gray walk out of the kitchen, then Zoe stood up. "I need air," she said.

"Okay. Come on, we'll go out on the deck," Maggie said.

She unlocked the sliding door and stepped out first, looked around. The grass beyond the deck started out a light yellow-green from the deck lights, then faded out into a circle of black. Zoe stepped out onto the deck behind her, and Maggie led her to the steps.

Once they'd both sat down, Maggie reached out and gave Zoe's hand a squeeze, then let it go."I know you're scared," she said.

Zoe opened her mouth to say something, then stopped. She twisted her hands on her knees and shook her head. She squeezed her eyes shut, then opened them again.

"I'm not scared. I'm…I just hate!" she said. "I just feel hate!"

Maggie watched her, let her say what she needed to say.

"He smiled at me! He smiled right at me, touching my food and…smiling!" she spat out. "He made me sick."

"I know," Maggie said.

Zoe whipped her head around. "He shoved a bunch of leaves in me. Did you know that?"

"Yes."

"Like I was a trash bag or something, like I wasn't even a human being," Zoe said. "I keep thinking about him standing there, smiling at me like he was a normal person, and I want to stab him in the face!"

Maggie waited. Zoe lifted her hands from her knees.

"My hands are shaking, I hate him so much!"

Maggie reached out for Zoe's hands, but the girl jerked them away. "No!"

"I can't stand feeling so much hate, but at least I'm not standing in the corner like a baby! I don't want it to stop!"

Zoe looked away, up into the trees in the wooded lot next door.

Maggie stood up and walked down the steps. Zoe watched her as she opened the doors of a low shed beneath the deck, and pulled out a softball hitting stick. The bright yellow-green knob at the end had seen better seasons, and was patched with duct tape. Maggie reached into the shed and rummaged through a few aluminum bats before pulling out one of the dark, wooden Louisville Sluggers that had belonged to her late husband.

"Come on," she said quietly to Zoe, and started walking away from the deck. After a moment, she heard Zoe descend the deck steps.

Maggie stopped in the middle of the well-lit circle and turned around. Zoe stopped a few feet away, looking unsure. Maggie bopped the end of the batting stick against the ground a few times.

"Remember this?" she asked Zoe.

"Yeah," the girl said.

Maggie held out the wooden bat. "Aluminum bats suck. Nothing feels as good as swinging a wooden bat," she said, as Zoe reached out and took it. "That was my husband David's. Do you remember him?"

Zoe nodded. "Yeah, Coach."

"He could really swing," Maggie said. She spread her feet a little, dug in, and raised the batting stick. "Let's go. Let's see what you got in there."

Zoe looked at her a moment, then got into something of a batting stance. She swung once and missed, then immediately swung a second time and connected, but Maggie barely felt it.

"Come on, swing all the way through," Maggie said. Zoe took another swing. "Again."

Zoe widened her stance a little, swung again, connected.

"Come on, Zoe," Maggie said, not unkindly. "Get your weight on that back foot. Bend your knees."

Zoe dug her back foot in a bit, swung again, hit a little bit harder.

"Swing with your hips, not your arms."

"I am," Zoe said, frustrated. She swung again but grazed the target.

Maggie raised the end of the batting stick up to Zoe's eye level. "See this?"

"Yeah?"

"Smiling right in your face!" She slammed the end of the stick onto the ground a couple of times, then held it up for Zoe. "Use your hips. All your power in your hips. Do it again."

Zoe swung again, and Maggie felt the hit speed up the length of the stick and vibrate in her shoulder muscles.

"Good. Do it again."

Zoe swung again, and grunted as she connected with the target.

"Again."

The wooden bat thumped against the end of the batting stick over and over and over. Occasionally, Zoe grunted with the effort, but Maggie said nothing else.

In the open sliding glass door, Gray stood and watched, his hands in his pajama pockets, the breeze blowing his graying hair into his eyes.

The Florida Seafood Festival was in full flux when Maggie and her family arrived in the early afternoon. Thousands of people were in attendance, and Battery Park was virtually unrecognizable. There were rows of vendor booths set up, selling every variation of local seafood, snacks tee shirts, beer, and other drinks. Many of the booths were donating proceeds to local charities; all were doing a brisk business.

The air was filled with music from the concert stage, announcements over the loudspeaker about the day's schedule, and the sounds of children shouting to each other and parents shouting at them. On the bay side, carnival rides blared out their own music, accompanied by the screams and laughter of the people riding them.

The day was bright and dry and fairly cool; a perfect Saturday for this, the largest annual event in Apalach.

Maggie stayed by Zoe's side throughout the afternoon, except for the few times when the girl was persuaded to ride something with Sky and Kyle. Maggie didn't do rides that left the ground, but she waited and watched until Zoe was back on the ground and back by her side. Maggie watched as Zoe sometimes seemed to be able to forget for a few moments that her life had changed. She watched as she always, eventually, remembered, and her eyes looked tired again. She also watched as she saw Zoe watching, her eyes darting and her head turning as she surveyed the crowds, searching for bleached blond hair.

Wyatt joined them only now and then, as he was essentially working, helping Sheriff's and Apalach PD officers with crowd control and lost kids, misplaced wallets, and misplaced sobriety.

He stood with an arm around Maggie's shoulder as they all watched Kyle participate in the kids' crab races. Maggie always felt bad for the crabs. Five minutes of people screaming at them, and then even the winner went into some vendor's pot.

She followed her parents, Sky, and Zoe as they went to congratulate Kyle on his 2nd place win, and John Solomon took Maggie's place at Wyatt's side.

"Hey, Wyatt," John said.

"Hey, John," Wyatt said.

John had been with the Sheriff's Office for twenty years before he'd retired to become the Executive Director of the Chamber of Commerce. The Seafood Festival was his baby, and the high point of his entire year.

"If you want some of my fried oysters, you better get over there pretty soon," John said.

John's third love, after his family and the festival, was cooking. Every fundraising event in Franklin County featured John at a grill or a fryer.

Wyatt sighed. "How long have we known each other, John?" Wyatt said.

"Uh, let's see...ten years?"

"And we have some variation of this conversation every year," Wyatt said. "I can't stand oysters."

"Oh, yeah," John said, frowning. "I guess I just like you so much that I keep forgetting you're a moron."

Wyatt grimaced at him, and John gave him a wink, then took a drink of his bottled water.

"Good crowd this year," he said. "New record."

"It always is," Wyatt said. "You did good."

"Team effort, my friend. Team effort," John said. "Hey, I saw the thing in the paper the other day. I didn't actually believe you were gonna do it, man."

"Yep," Wyatt said.

"Good for you."

Wyatt raised his plastic cup of Mountain Dew at him. "You got any advice?"

"Yeah, don't sleep with the detectives," John said, smiling.

"I've never slept with Terry," Wyatt said.

"I'm sure his wife appreciates that," John said.

"For the record, I'm not sleeping with Maggie, either."

"No offense, my friend," John said.

"None taken," Wyatt said. "We're doing the old-fashioned thing."

"Crap, Wyatt. Are y'all getting married?"

"If I can get her to hurry up and ask," Wyatt said.

"That's awesome, man," John said, patting him on the back. "That makes me happy."

"Thanks."

"So do you know who they're putting in your office yet?"

"Nope," Wyatt answered. "I'm meeting the suits in Tallahassee Monday."

"Nobody's gonna like him," John said.

"So I hear. I've never felt more loved," Wyatt said.

John smiled, then looked past him. "Penny's rubber-necking for me," he said, speaking of his wife. "Back to work. I'll see you around."

"See you later," Wyatt said, as John hurried away. A few moments later, Maggie came back.

"I'm gonna take Zoe back to my folks'," she said.

"Already?" Wyatt asked. "It's only four o'clock."

"Yeah, but she's done," Maggie said. "Hyper-vigilance is exhausting."

Wyatt frowned and nodded. "Your parents going, too?"

Maggie grinned at him. "Please. Daddy hasn't missed an oyster shucking contest yet. Or lost one."

"All right. Well, I'll talk to you later," Wyatt said.

"Okay," Maggie said.

Wyatt glanced around, then yanked on her hand, pulled her in for a quick kiss. "We can do crap like that now," he said.

CHAPTER

TWENTY-FOUR

aggie and Zoe sat in a pair of Adirondack chairs in the back yard, in front of Daddy's new fire pit. The wood crackled and spit, and the fire did a spasmodic dance as the evening breeze hit it. It was Maggie's favorite part of the day, when sunset and dark kissed very briefly in the sky.

"So, Wyatt's your boyfriend?" Zoe asked.

"Yes," Maggie said, and felt embarrassed by the warmth in her face. Zoe didn't seem to notice.

"Does he know about what happened to you?"

"Yes."

"And he doesn't care? It doesn't matter?" Zoe asked.

Maggie looked over at Zoe. "No."

"Did your husband know?"

"No," Maggie said again. She shifted in her seat, faced Zoe. "And whether you decide to tell somebody in the future, that's up to you," she said. "But a good man will know that rape has nothing to do with sex."

Zoe nodded. "That's kind of what Sky says, too," she said after a moment.

"She's wise sometimes," Maggie said.

Zoe gave her half a smile. "She's cool." She stood up then, and stretched her back. "I have to use the restroom."

Maggie smiled at her, then looked out at the almost invisible silver of the bay as she heard Zoe go up the deck stairs and slide open the door. She couldn't see the bay well, but she could smell it, and she took a long, slow drink of it. She was thinking about healing, hers and Zoe's, and about how a place can help you do that, when the skin on the back of her neck heated up, and the hairs on arms became electrically charged.

She was already leaning forward in her chair when she heard a gentle rustling, had already pulled her weapon from the back of her jeans when she started standing, but she didn't manage to turn all the way around. The piece of firewood struck her in the right temple, and she continued spinning as she fell backward.

She heard it hit before she felt it, and saw his bleached hair glowing against the dark sky behind him as she fell. The ground slammed into her like it had been running at her. The pain hit her then, in the temple and in the back of her head, and she felt her gun skitter out of her hand, heard a metallic *clang* as white light exploded behind her eyes.

The light faded, and the dark came back into focus, just as she saw him raise the piece of firewood over his head. She rolled to the side, heard it come down behind her, thumping the ground just six inches from her head.

She rolled again, onto her stomach, and was almost on her hands and knees when his foot struck her right side. She rolled again, this time not of her own volition. It hurt, and it took the wind out of her, but she felt a flash of gratitude that he obviously wasn't wearing boots.

She landed face down, and rolled onto her back just as he dropped, his knees on either side of her. Her head spun, and his head spun with it. She saw two of his faces, and both of them looked more frightened than angry, though the anger was there, too.

"This is none of your business!" he spat out, his eyes wide.

Maggie's arms felt oddly heavy as she lifted them to cover her head. She was a moment too slow, and his fist connected with her cheek.

"This is between me and her!" he yelled.

Maggie just had time to think that she was going to get up, and she was going to kill him when she did, then she heard Zoe's voice from somewhere that sounded further away than it probably was.

"Get *off* of her!" Zoe screamed.

Maggie heard a dull thump, heard Finch grunt, and then felt him leave her. Maggie's face expanded and contracted as she blinked her eyes rapidly, willing herself not to lose consciousness.

She heard another thump.

"Zoe!" she heard Finch yell.

Another thump, and Maggie heard Finch groan.

"Get *away* from us!" Maggie heard Zoe yell.

Thump.

Maggie rolled onto her right side. Zoe was standing over Finch, who was getting to his hands and knees.

"Smile at me," Zoe yelled. "Smile at me!"

Zoe swung David's beautiful wooden bat once again, and caught Finch in the ribs. Maggie noticed, crazily, that Zoe was swinging from the hips.

Finch landed on his back and put up a hand. "Zoe," he said, his voice weaker.

Zoe swung again, hit the hand dead on, and Finch screamed and dropped his arm.

"Smile at me again!" Zoe yelled, and the bat got him in the side of the knee.

Maggie rolled over, scrambled over to the fire pit. Her gun had skittered beneath it, and she reached for it, gasped as the back of her hand made contact with the scorching bottom of the fire pit. She yanked her hand back out and scrambled to her feet.

Her head spun a moment, then she ran the few steps between her and Zoe, who was getting ready for another swing.

"Zoe!" Maggie yelled.

Zoe swung, but lost her momentum as she looked over her shoulder. Finch grabbed the bat out of her hands and threw it over his head.

Maggie swung her arm around and leveled her weapon at Finch's face. He threw his hands up.

"I'm not armed!" he gasped.

Maggie didn't take her finger from the Glock's double trigger.

"Leave us alone!" he yelled. "This is between her and me!"

Maggie felt bile rising up in her throat. "The only thing between you and her is me."

⚓　⚓　⚓

Finch had been taken to the ER via ambulance and Maggie had been taken via Wyatt. It took the ER doctor a little under an hour to put three stitches in Maggie's temple, check her for concussion, ice down her cheek, and pronounce her fit to leave. Zoe held her hand the entire time, as Wyatt watched from a spot on the wall, arms folded over his chest.

Finch was taken to Franklin County Jail, Maggie was taken back to her parents' house. Now, three hours later, she sat at the table on the deck, staring at the embers of the fire she and Zoe had built before sunset, and drinking coffee her mother had made. Maggie's parents had gone to bed, but Wyatt sat at the table, Mountain Dew in hand.

Zoe, Sky, and Kyle sat on the deck stairs talking quietly.

"I'm thinking if Piggly-Wiggly doesn't hire you, we could start a charter fishing business," Wyatt said quietly.

Maggie looked at him and smiled. It hurt her cheek. Wyatt's tone was light, but she saw the stress and exhaustion in his eyes. "I'm kind of offended that you think they won't take me," she said.

"Maybe if you wait until your face heals," he said.

"Maybe."

Maggie looked back at the kids as Kyle got up from the steps and walked out into the yard, his Nautica pajama bottoms dragging through the dew that had already appeared. He walked out of the circle of light into the dark, bent over, then came back with his father's Louisville slugger.

He stopped in front of the girls and they ceased their talking. "This is supposed to be mine, but Dad had three more. You should have this one," Kyle said quietly.

Zoe hesitated a moment, then reached out and took it. "Thanks," she said quietly.

Kyle sat back down on the steps, and Maggie looked over at Wyatt.

"You should know that he told me today that he might marry her," Wyatt said in a hushed voice.

Maggie looked over at the kids and smiled. "She deserves him," she said.

⚓ ⚓ ⚓

The next afternoon, Maggie stood by her mother's car as her father loaded luggage into the trunk.

Gray had decided everyone needed to get away for a few days, school or no school, and they were taking the kids to Destin. Maggie had been cowardly about calling Paulette for permission, and was still trying to figure out if she owed the woman an apology, so Gray had called her.

"I still wish you were coming, Sunshine," Gray said, as he rearranged things in the cramped trunk.

"Me, too, Daddy," Maggie said. "But I have to work tomorrow, and Wyatt and I are going to have dinner. He's heading out to Tallahassee tonight so he doesn't have to leave at dark-thirty tomorrow morning."

"Even so," Gray said. "You could use a little break."

"That's the truth, Daddy," Maggie said.

She heard kids' voices, and turned around to look over at the front porch. Kyle and Zoe were looking at something on Kyle's phone.

"I think Kyle's got his first crush," Maggie said.

"He could do worse," Gray said.

"Yep." Maggie watched them for a moment. "I was thinking...I was thinking about asking Wyatt what he thought about keeping her."

Gray looked over his shoulder at her. "That a fact?"

"Well, yeah. I mean, I *should* ask him." Maggie swallowed. "If we're going to be, you know, married eventually. What do you think?"

"Well, I'll tell you what," Gray said. "It's a noble idea, but I talked to Zoe somewhat the other night, and she loves her aunt."

"I'm sure she does," Maggie said, almost defensively.

"And her aunt loves her, in the way she knows how," Gray said. "Zoe feels that if she leaves, her aunt won't have any reason to turn things around."

"She's fourteen," Maggie said. "It's not her responsibility to help her aunt get clean."

"No, but she feels it anyway," Gray said. "She's just trying to hang on to the one piece of family she's got left." He straightened up, grabbed another small suitcase, and jammed it into the space he'd made. "So consider that, and make sure that whatever you do, you do it for her, not for you."

Maggie swallowed. "Do you think I'm being selfish?"

Gray straightened up again, the suitcase half in and half out. "No, I think you feel as responsible for her happiness as she does for her aunt's. Maggie, you've been bringing home every stray dog, run-over turtle and mangy cat since you could walk. It's what you do."

Maggie looked over at Zoe, then back at her father. "I just want her to be safe," she said.

"I know that. And if she wants to come live with you, then y'all should do that." He bent back over the trunk and finished stuffing the suitcase in. "Wyatt can handle it," he said. "It doesn't take a saint to raise another man's child, Maggie."

Maggie saw his hands go still on the suitcase, watched his hands as they busied themselves again in a moment, checking that the suitcase was zipped.

"In any event," Gray said, "Wyatt's already planning to do that with Sky and Kyle."

"Yeah," Maggie said.

Gray stood up, then carefully closed the trunk. He turned around and looked at her, then looked over her shoulder. "Here comes your mama with another bag," he said.

He looked back at her, and she squinted up into his eyes, those gentle brown eyes that Maggie felt held all the kindness and wisdom in the world.

"I love you, Sunshine," he said.

"I love you, too, Daddy," she said back.

TWENTY-FIVE

M aggie went home to feed the chickens and Coco and
Stoopid.

She was happy to see them, and wrapped her
arms around Coco's vibrating neck for a moment,
inhaling her fur and her adoration, but there was a weight
in her chest that she couldn't ignore. A dread and a growing sense of sadness that felt a lot like impending loss.

Coco gave Maggie her "go-with" face when Maggie
packed an overnight bag and started to leave, but Maggie
decided to leave her there. Stoopid wasn't much of a rooster at the moment, with his idiotic cone and his drip bottle
of water, and someone needed to watch over things. Maggie also felt a need to be alone.

Wyatt had suggested that Maggie sleep at his house that
night.

"Is this another one of those over-protective things
where you whine about me living out in the wild?" Maggie had asked him.

"No, this is one of those testosterone-driven things where it makes me feel all macho and proprietary because you're in my house while I'm gone," he'd said.

She and Wyatt had a quiet dinner on his back patio, then she followed him out to the driveway as he got ready to leave. He tossed his bag in the passenger seat of his truck, shut the door, then turned around to look at her.

"The spare key is taped under the grill," he said.

"What kind of Sheriff leaves a key on the back patio?" she asked him.

"What kind of burglar thinks a Sheriff would do something that stupid?" he asked back.

She smiled at him, and he smiled back, but then the smile faded. She saw him looking at the bruise on her cheek.

"I'll give you a good reference for Piggly-Wiggly," he said quietly.

"Okay," she said. He stared at her, and she grew uncomfortable. "Stop looking so serious."

"Stop looking so sad," he said. "What's on your mind?"

Maggie looked away. "Nothing. I'm just worn out."

Wyatt took a moment to answer. "Okay, we'll leave it at that, despite the fact that it's untrue." He put his hands on her face. "You'll tell when you're ready."

Maggie nodded, and covered his hands with hers. She wanted him to stay. She wanted him to hurry up and go.

"I'll be back tomorrow afternoon," Wyatt said.

"Okay." She looked up at him. "I love you, you know."

"I don't blame you," he said, but he wasn't smiling. "I love you, too."

Maggie worked up a smile, then he kissed her goodbye.

She stood in his driveway for a few minutes after he'd pulled away. A sense of aloneness settled in around her, and she was a little sorry she hadn't brought Coco. Or even Stoopid.

She walked out to the back patio, carried the last of the dishes into the kitchen, and washed them by hand even though Wyatt had a dishwasher. She looked out the window as she washed, stared out at nothing in particular, and thought.

She wiped down the counters, distractedly wiped down the patio table, swept the kitchen floor, and thought.

She sat out back, in the porch swing where she and Wyatt had been sitting just a short while before. She stared out at the night, so many snippets of the last few months and the last few days swirling and drifting around in her head, and the growing sadness was joined by fear.

She got down next to the grill, felt for the key, and pulled it out. Then she sat back down on the swing and turned it over and over in her hands, trying to forget about leaving, trying to get up the courage to do it.

If she walked out that door, she would lose someone she loved. She wasn't sure who. But it would break her heart.

⚓   ⚓   ⚓

Maggie stood in Boudreaux's driveway for several minutes. The palm trees rattled in the wind, but everything else was quiet.

She breathed deeply and slowly, afraid to move forward, unwilling to run away. One way or another, everything was about to change, and for one of any number of possible reasons, she would mourn that change. But she knew, in the part of her that was willing to admit unwelcome truth, that this moment had been ushered on its way the first time she'd walked up this driveway last summer.

Finally, she pulled her cell phone out of her back pocket and dialed.

"Hello?" he answered smoothly on the second ring.

"Hello, Mr. Boudreaux," Maggie said.

"Hello, Maggie," he said.

"I wasn't sure if you were still up," she said. "I was wondering if I could come by."

He hesitated for a moment. "I'm still up," he said. "Where are you?"

"In your driveway."

"I'm on the back porch," he said.

Maggie couldn't think of anything else to say so she hung up. She took a deep breath and headed down the oyster shell path that led to the back yard. When she turned the corner, he was standing at the porch rail near the steps. He turned to look at her, watched her approach. He was wearing a pair of khaki trousers and an aqua blue chambray shirt that matched his eyes.

"I didn't hear your car," he said.

"I walked. I'm spending the night at Wyatt's," she said.

"I see," he said quietly, then stood back as she came up the stairs.

When she stepped onto the porch, she watched him see her face. His was without expression.

"What happened?" he asked her quietly.

"We arrested the rapist I was looking for last night," she said.

"I heard about the arrest, but I didn't know you'd been hurt."

"It's not that bad," she said.

She was surprised when he reached out and touched her cheek with one finger, as gently as a leaf falling. She watched as his jaw tensed almost imperceptibly, saw his eyes grow cold for just a moment as he touched her chin and turned her head so he could look at her tiny stitches. Then he looked her in the eye, and the coldness was gone.

"Does Wyatt know you're here?"

"No. He's on his way to Tallahassee," she said.

He looked at her a moment. "And you're here," he said.

"Yes." She felt self-conscious, and looked over at the French doors that led to his office. They were open, and the white sheers drifted back and forth against the porch floor. She looked back at him. "Have I ever told you that you have a very calming effect on me?" she asked.

He smiled. "I think you're the only person who's ever said that to me," he said.

She smiled back and shrugged. "Strange but true."

"Do you need calming?" he asked her, his smile gone again.

"I feel like smiling," she said. "I feel like forgetting about everything out there, and just…enjoying a few moments of peace."

"Well. Then I'm honored that you came here," he said. "I was thinking about having a glass of wine. Would you like one?"

Maggie thought about that. "Actually, I could use something stronger."

He nodded. "Okay." He put a hand on her arm. "It's a little chilly out here for that blouse you're wearing. Why don't we go inside?"

She followed him into the den, stopped just inside as he went to the bar.

"What would you like?" he asked.

"A shot of tequila would be nice, actually," she said.

He hesitated a moment, then nodded. "Shots of tequila, then."

She watched him as he got out two shot glasses and a bottle of tequila. It looked expensive, but she wouldn't know, really. She hadn't done shots since she and David had accidentally gone to Shreveport during Mardi Gras.

"Excuse me just a moment," Boudreaux said, then went back out to the porch. She looked out, saw him open the mini-fridge. He came back with a lime in his hand. "We might as well do it correctly," he said as he passed her.

She watched him slice the lime, then he beckoned to her. She walked over to the bar, and he took her hand, rubbed a wedge of lime on the back of it, and handed her a salt shaker. She took it and shook a bit of salt onto her hand. He did the same with a piece of lime of his own, then handed her a shot glass.

She took it, waited for him to take his, then they raised their glasses. "To smiling," he said, and licked his hand. She did the same, and they downed their shots. Maggie had to force the last bit of it down, and thought about dying once she had, but after sucking on the lime for a second, she welcomed the sudden rush of warmth in her chest and stomach.

Boudreaux smiled at her as he put down his glass. "Would you like some water?" he asked her.

"Actually, I think I'd like one more," she said.

"Are you sure?" he asked her, frowning. "What do you weigh, a hundred pounds?"

"Somewhere around there," she said. "It's okay."

He looked at her a moment, then held his hand out for her glass. "Okay, if you say so," he said. He put it down on the bar and opened the tequila bottle again. "Maybe it'll loosen you up enough to tell me what's wrong."

Maggie smiled, mostly. "Thank you," she said noncommittally.

They drank their second shot, and that one went down more easily for Maggie. She handed him her glass and ate the slice of lime in her hand. When she looked around for a trash can, he held out his hand. She gave it to him, and he tossed it in a small dish on the bar.

"Would you like to sit down?" he asked her.

She nodded, and he led her to the loveseat facing the window. She sat, and was surprised when he sat down beside her, at a respectful distance but not very far away. He watched her for a moment. She was feeling slightly bolder than usual suddenly, and she held his gaze.

"I slept in here the other night," she said.

"In here?" he asked.

"Yes. I was restless and lonely and I couldn't sleep, so I came down here. I slept in your sweater, actually," she said, and she was less embarrassed by that than she normally would be. She smiled. "I hope you don't mind."

"I don't," he said.

"I feel safe with you," she said.

Those insanely blue eyes stared into hers, and she felt like he could see through to the other side of her. "You are safe with me," he said quietly.

"I know," she said. "Your sweater made me feel safe, too. I know that's silly."

"No, it's not," he said. "It's actually very touching." She smiled at him, and he gave her a smile back. "Feel free to borrow the sweater any time you like."

"Thank you. I'll wear it on my next date with Wyatt," she said.

He laughed then, and Maggie realized it was the first time she'd ever seen him laugh fully, laugh like he meant it. It made her quietly proud. It also made her sad, but less so than she had been thirty minutes ago. She didn't care for being drunk, but she was grateful right then, for the buzz.

Boudreaux looked at her. "Are you ready to talk about whatever is weighing on you?"

"Let's talk about something else," she said. "Let's talk about good things."

"Very well. What would you like to talk about?"

Maggie came up blank. She just wanted a little bit of time. Looking at him there, smiling, relaxed, she just wanted a little bit of time to enjoy being with him. To have things the way they had been, before they became something else.

"Tell me something about you that I don't know," she said then. "I don't mean some deep, dark secret. Just something that would surprise me."

He smiled at her, leaned his head back against the back of the loveseat. "Something you don't know," he said to the ceiling, then he turned and looked at her. "Not deep and dark."

He grinned at her, and she realized with some surprise that he was a little buzzed as well. She didn't know if she felt guilty or relieved.

"Okay," he said. He thought a moment, stared back up at the ceiling, then looked back at her and winked. "On occasion, I still listen to disco."

That did take her by surprise, and she laughed. "No, you don't."

"Oh, Maggie," he said, smiling. "It hurts me when you question my integrity."

"I believe you have integrity," she said, laughing. "I just don't believe you listen to disco."

"Oh, *cher*," he said. "Cajuns love three things. We love to eat, we love to laugh, and we love to dance."

"I know you love to dance," she said. "I danced with you at the Cajun festival."

"We danced indeed," he said. "But there was a time, way back when, that I stayed at the clubs all night, so that

I could dance to disco. Terrible music, really, but so much fun to dance to."

"I don't believe you," she said teasingly.

He grinned at her. "Cajuns also love a dare."

He got up and walked over to a mahogany bookcase. There was an expensive and complicated-looking stereo system on the top shelf, and he opened a small case next to it and started fingering through a row of CDs.

"Let's see here," he said to himself. "Ah. This will do nicely."

He opened the case, slid the CD into the player, then turned and smiled as he walked back toward her. "I'll expect an apology."

He held out a hand as the music began. Maggie recognized the melody, but couldn't place the song. "What is that?" she asked.

"'I Love the Nightlife' by Alicia Bridges,'" he said. He snapped his fingers. "Let's go."

Maggie smiled and stood up. "I don't know anything about disco," she said.

"Can you samba?" he asked, as he led her to the middle of the room.

"Yes."

"Then we're good," he said.

Maggie had been surprised, those months ago, to find that Boudreaux was a fine dancer, but she was surprised yet again. He was too much of a gentleman to out-dance her so badly that she couldn't keep up, but he was clearly in his element.

They danced, they twirled, and they laughed, and Maggie found herself forgetting about anything that wasn't in that room. They ended up dancing to three songs, none of which Maggie knew, and finally collapsed back onto the loveseat. Once they'd stopped laughing and caught their breath, he looked over at her.

"My apology," he said.

"I apologize, Mr. Boudreaux," she said formally.

"And we will never speak of this outside this room," he said. "It'll weaken my reputation."

She smiled at him, then dropped her head onto the back of the loveseat and let out a huge breath. "Disco is rough," she said.

"What kind of music do you listen to?" he asked her.

"Gosh. A lot of different stuff," she said. "It depends on my mood. I like The Civil Wars a lot."

"I listen to a lot of different music, but I've never heard of The Civil Wars," he said.

"They're beautiful," she said, then arched her back so she could get her phone out of her pocket. Boudreaux watched her curiously as she flicked through her playlists.

"What's your favorite song?" he asked her.

"Uh….that's hard," she said. "But 'Poison & Wine' is right up there."

"Play it for me," he said.

She looked at him. "If I do, will you slow dance with me?"

"A gentleman would never say no," he answered quietly.

Maggie smiled, tried to ignore a sudden, small but noticeable creeping of regret seeping past her buzz. "Okay."

She clicked on the song, then turned the volume all the way up as Boudreaux stood and held out his hand.

He walked her back to the middle of the room as the music began, then drew her to him, close to himself, but respectfully so. She put her free hand around his shoulder, let the phone rest against his back as they began to dance.

They were quiet for a moment as the music played, sweet and haunting. Maggie felt his warmth, smelled his quietly elegant cologne, and realized that she felt the sadness creeping back, but also comfort. She wanted the physical contact. She was a naturally affectionate person, prone to hugging and holding people she cared about. She realized, not really surprised, that she cared deeply for this man. She had known it for some time, known it because of her desire to spend time with him, known it because of her reluctance to stay away, even for Wyatt. But she hadn't necessarily recognized that it was genuine caring, more so than any fascination.

She swallowed, as she felt her pleasant numbness slip away.

"This is lovely," Boudreaux said, very close to her ear. "The song."

"Yes," she said quietly.

"Sad, but haunting," he said after a moment.

"Yes," she said again.

His hand pressed gently against the small of her back, and she rested her good cheek against his shoulder. She felt their evening slipping away, and she thought about leaving without doing what had brought her here. She just wanted this. Safety, comfort, familiarity.

She blinked a few times as her eyes warmed and moistened, then closed them altogether and let herself rest against him. She listened to his quiet, steady breathing more than she did the song, and was almost surprised when it ended.

"Thank you," he said, stepping back a bit as the room went quiet.

"Thank you," she said, and had to look away, out through the French doors.

"Do you mind if we step outside?" he asked her. "I'm ready for a cigarette."

She followed him outside, momentarily distracted from herself as she watched him take a pack of cigarettes from a small drawer in a side table.

"I didn't know you smoked," she said.

"I don't," he answered. "I quit almost twenty years ago. But every night, I have just one. Will it bother you?"

"No."

He leaned back against the porch rail, bent his head as he lit the cigarette and gently blew out the first plume. Maggie wondered at the control it took for a smoker to smoke just one cigarette a day, but she wasn't all that taken aback that Boudreaux could manage it. He was ever in control.

"This was the only way I could quit," he said. "Every night, once everyone else is in bed, I come out here and have one cigarette. It's when I'm at my most relaxed."

"You usually seem pretty relaxed," Maggie said, leaning beside him.

"I generally am, when I'm with you." He smiled. "The calming influence is mutual."

Maggie smiled. She wanted to go back to ten minutes ago, half an hour. "You weren't very calm when I was pointing a shotgun at you."

He laughed softly. "You didn't feel very safe with me then, either."

She looked into those eyes, and wished she could let herself leave. "A lot of things changed during that hurricane," she said.

"Yes," he said quietly.

He held her gaze, and she thought about shutting up. She thought about running. His hand was just a few inches from hers on the porch rail. They were standing almost close enough to dance, and she wished they could.

"You know, Wyatt worries about me, being with you," she said slowly.

"I know," he said. "Of course he does, but he doesn't need to." He took another draw on his cigarette, blew it away from her.

"I think Daddy worries that you're my latest injured turtle or lost cat."

He watched her as he took another drag. "I don't understand what that means," he said, then exhaled.

"It's a nurturing, rescuing thing," she said, shaking her head.

"Do you want to rescue me, Maggie?" he asked softly.

"Yes. Of course," she said. "I have. And you've rescued me."

He nodded. "Yes."

Maggie swallowed. "My mother just worries that I'm falling in love with you," she said, and instantly wanted to suck the words back in, but this was what she'd come here for. She watched something flicker in his eyes for a moment, just for an instant. Then he looked away and took a long drag of his cigarette. After a moment, he exhaled, then looked back at her.

"No, she doesn't," he said finally, sounding only slightly defensive.

"Why shouldn't she, Mr. Boudreaux?" Maggie asked. "You're extremely handsome and charismatic. You've done things…on my behalf. And you almost died saving my life. That's quite a heady combination."

He took one last, quick draw from his cigarette, then walked over to the side table, ground it out in the glass ashtray there. Maggie held her breath. She expected him to put distance between them, to sit down in the chair there, but he surprised her by turning around and walking back.

Boudreaux took a deep breath and walked back to the porch rail. He was unaccustomed to needing a moment to think, but this conversation was taking an unexpected turn. He'd like nothing more than to put her mind at ease about her family's concerns, but he wasn't prepared, at that moment, to do that honestly. Unfortunately, he couldn't think of a dishonest way to do it, either.

He leaned his hand back against the rail and looked at Maggie, waited.

"Haven't you ever considered it, Mr., Boudreaux?" she asked quietly.

"Considered what, Maggie? That your parents would think you were having an affair with me?"

"No," she said, and he thought she looked almost scared. "That I would want to."

Boudreaux stopped breathing for a moment, and he felt a chill move through his gut, like someone had opened up the scar that went across his midsection, and poured a glass of ice water into it.

"I don't think I've ever seen you look surprised, Mr. Boudreaux," she said softly. "When you first started this…relationship, did you really never think that might happen?"

"You're in love with Wyatt," he said after a moment, unable to think of something less impotent off the top of his head. No, he had not at any time considered that possibility.

"I wouldn't be the first woman to love one man and fall for another," she said. "I'm sure I wouldn't be the first one to fall for you."

Boudreaux's eyes narrowed just a bit, involuntarily. He stared at her, seeking out pretense or deceit, but all he saw was vulnerability, and maybe a little bit of fear.

"Maggie…" he started, then didn't know what he wanted to say.

"Would that be unwelcome, Mr. Boudreaux?" she asked, and he saw her lower lip tremble just slightly.

He swallowed. "It would be impossible," he said.

"Are you gay?" she asked him, and he heard hope in her voice.

"No," he answered quietly.

Her eyes instantly teared up, and she looked out at the dark yard. "The alcohol has worn off," she said quietly. "Enough for me to feel embarrassed."

"Maggie," he said, and she looked back at him. A tear streaked slowly down her bruised cheek, and he wondered how God could be so cruelly ironic, that He would put Boudreaux in the position of having to reassure his daughter that he didn't find her unattractive.

Then he thought that this was probably exactly the situation that his lies had earned him, exactly the penance he should face for having inserted himself into her life as he had.

"Maggie," he said softly. He reached out and touched a thumb to her cheek, gently wiped away the tear that slid alongside her nose. "Let me make something very clear. If we weren't who we are, if circumstances were different, I have no doubt that you would have been the one great love of my life."

Her eyes pooled again, and a tear slid down the other cheek. He dropped his hand, let it go.

"Which circumstances are those, Mr. Boudreaux?" she asked.

He let out a slow breath to keep himself from telling the truth. He had long since decided that that truth shouldn't come from him.

"All of them," he said finally.

She stared back at him for a moment, then nodded. "I need to go."

"I wish you wouldn't," he said, though he couldn't imagine where their night could go from here.

"I need to," she said, then shoved away from the railing.

"I'll walk you back to Wyatt's," he said, straightening up.

"No. It's okay," she said. "I'd really prefer you didn't."

They looked at each other a moment, and Boudreaux stopped himself from telling her to sit down and listen.

"Goodnight, Mr. Boudreaux," she said quietly.

"Goodnight, Maggie," he answered, and watched her walk down the steps, along the path, and around the corner of the house.

⚓ ⚓ ⚓

Maggie's boots crunched through the driveway and onto the sidewalk. It was only once she'd reached the concrete that Maggie allowed herself to breathe again.

She wished she had never come here. She wished she hadn't needed to know what she didn't want to know. She had known it was a risk. She had known that there were several bad ways that it could go tonight. She had known that she was going to lose someone she loved tonight, and it had been her friend and comforter, Bennett Boudreaux.

She had known that there was more than one answer that could hurt her.

Unfortunately, she'd gotten the one that would hurt the most. She hadn't wanted to be unfaithful to Wyatt, hadn't wanted Boudreaux to lean in and kiss her and declare his undying love. But she'd give anything right now if he had.

She made it to Wyatt's front door without giving in to the clenching she felt in her chest, managed to fumble the key into the lock before she gave way to the tightness in her throat and let out a sob that frightened her with its force. Then she slammed the door behind her.

Across the street, Bennett Boudreaux stood on the corner, his hands in his pants pockets and the wind sweeping his hair into his eyes. He stood there and watched the house for a moment, then turned and walked away.

A FEW WORDS OF
TH⚓NKS

Thank you to my patient and tireless editor, Tammi Labrecque of LarksandKatydids.com, to my wonderful cover designer, Shayne Rutherford of DarkMoonGraphics.com, and to book designer goddess Colleen Sheehan of WriteDreamRepeat.com. You are the trifecta of publishing.

Special thanks, as always, to my technical advisor and friend John Solomon, who shares his experience with the Franklin County Sheriff's Office, and his love of Apalach, so generously.

To my beautifully dysfunctional family of authors in Author's Corner: Thank you for your constant supply of encouragement, support, laughter, knowledge and tubesteak. I love you, each and every one.

Finally, to my children, Michael, Kat, Chelsey, Matthew and Rebecca; it is because of you that I write, and it is only because of you that I can.

Made in United States
North Haven, CT
16 September 2024

57519544R00124